YOURS TO LOVE

LANTERN BAY, BOOK 6

SOPHIE HAYDON

BAY BOOKS

Yours to Love
by Sophie Haydon

—The Mackenzies—
A Place Called Home
Secrets at Parata Bay
Escape to Shelter Springs
What you See in the Stars
Second Chance at Whisper Creek
Summer at the Lakehouse Café

—Lantern Bay—
Yours to Give
Yours to Treasure
Yours to Cherish
Yours to Keep
Yours Forever
Yours to Love

For more information about this author, visit:
https://sophiehaydon.com

© 2022 Sophie Haydon
ISBN 978-1-99-102119-9 (epub)
ISBN 978-1-99-102139-7 (Amazon Print edn)
ISBN 978-1-99-102135-9 (Draft2Digital Print edn)

CONTENTS

Chapter 1	1
Chapter 2	16
Chapter 3	33
Chapter 4	49
Chapter 5	66
Chapter 6	81
Chapter 7	94
Chapter 8	108
Chapter 9	122
Chapter 10	135
Chapter 11	152
Chapter 12	165
Epilogue	183
Afterword	189
Summer at the Lakehouse Café	191
Also by Sophie Haydon	195

"A lantern glowing and stars looking down, and the sea smells blowing."
— **Cicely Fox Smith**

*C*harlotte Kincaid squinted at the screen of her phone, blinked, and brought it closer to her face. It couldn't be.

"What's up?" asked Rachel, taking a sip of her wine, oblivious to the glances in their direction from the other patrons of the Christchurch wine bar.

"I'm not sure," said Charlotte, reaching into her Birkin bag for the glasses she rarely used in public. "It looks to be a message from…" She trailed off, biting her lip. What on earth could have made her father text her? She slipped on her glasses and re-read the message twice before she allowed herself to believe the ridiculously lengthy message, complete with perfect punctuation. Her father had always been a stickler for doing things correctly.

She placed the phone carefully on the table and looked up at Rachel. "William is coming for Christmas."

Rachel frowned. "Who is William, and why is he coming to yours for Christmas?"

"William is my father, and I'm not sure why he's coming for Christmas. He's never come before when I've asked him."

"You call your father William?"

"Everybody does."

"You mean, no one ever called him Dad, or at least Father, to you? Not even your mum?"

"Goodness, no!" She smiled as she imagined anyone calling her very formal and aloof father by such a familiar name.

"How come?"

Charlotte shrugged. "He's not that kind of man, I guess. He's a High Court Judge in Wellington and few people call him by his first name. At work he's 'The Right Honorable Justice Dempsey', to acquaintances he's 'sir' and to his closest friends he's William."

Rachel's frown deepened. "But not Father. Never Father?"

Charlotte shook her head. "Never." She pondered on the matter for a moment. She was so used to it that she'd never really questioned it. "I guess he's not really a family man."

"That's tough for his only child, then."

Charlotte didn't answer this time. Because Rachel was right. It *had* been tough, and it still was.

"So," continued Rachel, obviously realizing she'd touched a raw nerve. "Why is this so unexpected? It would be unexpected for us Connellys *not* to be with Dad for Christmas."

"Yes, well, we don't all have families like the Connellys. I usually spend Christmas at the Christchurch City Mission."

Rachel raised an eyebrow. "I bet you're the only helper wearing a designer outfit."

"They're just jeans," said Charlotte, suddenly embarrassed, wondering what the others might think of her. "I guess they are designer jeans, though," she mumbled.

"You know you're always welcome to celebrate Christmas at Belendroit."

"I don't like to intrude."

"I know, but you won't be intruding. I promise." Charlotte

felt uncomfortable under Rachel's thoughtful gaze. "And I also know you don't like to be on your own. Ever." Charlotte winced. She wished she hadn't confided this weakness to her friend.

She gave Rachel a quick, forced smile. "I guess I'm not the only one." She looked away again as her thoughts strayed to the only time she was ever alone. At night. When she found it hard to sleep.

"But back to the fascinating subject of your father," said Rachel, sensitive as usual to the moods of others. "Have you invited him to visit you before?"

"Yes, of course! I invite him every year and every year without fail he declines. But..." She glanced at her phone and re-checked her message. Yep, it hadn't changed. "For some reason, this year he's accepted. I can't believe it."

"Well," said Rachel, obviously struggling to understand what that must feel like. "I guess it's going to be a great Christmas!"

"Yes, I guess it is." Then it came to her, and she let out the kind of expletive she only ever heard everyone but her say. She followed it up with a wail which turned a few more heads their way.

"What is it?"

"Oh, no!" Charlotte rubbed her forehead. "I know why he's coming!"

"Why?"

"To meet my fiancé."

"Fiancé? You have a fiancé? This is the first I've heard of it!"

Charlotte shifted uncomfortably in her seat. To all the world, she was the woman who had everything, and that was how she liked it. But to her father, she always seemed to lack something. "Every time my father contacts me, he asks me when I'm going to get married. And, well, I'd had a few glasses of wine last time he asked and I told him I had a fiancé."

"Why on earth did you feel you had to tell him that?"

Charlotte shrugged as if she didn't know. But she did.

"Charlotte?" said Rachel, in a mock-threatening tone. "Why?"

Charlotte frowned as she searched for an explanation which would satisfy Rachel. "My father is..." She shrugged again. "Difficult to please."

"Hm," said Rachel, sitting back in her seat but continuing to observe Charlotte in a way which made her uncomfortable. Like all the Connellys, Rachel had an unnerving ability to read people accurately. "So your father isn't pleased that you gained a first class honors degree, followed by a PhD in law at Oxford University?"

Charlotte remembered her father's indifference and how he'd failed to turn up to any of her graduation ceremonies.

"Or that you're the only person I know who has no taint of scandal, who has never put a foot wrong, who has, in fact, led a model life of industry and integrity?"

"I'm beginning to think a scandal would have piqued his interest more than the lack of one." She sighed and took a sip of her wine.

"Right," said Rachel. "And so you invented a fiancé."

Charlotte mumbled her reply, taking another hasty sip.

"And you don't have a fiancé."

Charlotte shook her head and sighed. "Rachel, what on earth am I going to do?"

"Tell him the truth, maybe? Say, Dad, or in your case, William, I made up the fiancé bit to please you, but I now realize I've gone a step too far and need to tell you there is no such person."

Charlotte felt the color drain from her face at the thought of saying any such thing. "I can't tell my father I lied."

"Why not? Being the perfect daughter hasn't helped you so far, has it?"

Charlotte couldn't argue with that.

Rachel leaned forward and took hold of Charlotte's hands. "Charlotte, does your father's approval really still mean so much to you?"

Charlotte nodded. "It does. I know it shouldn't. But it does. I feel like there's a big hole inside which needs to be filled by his approval and love."

"You think he doesn't love you?" Charlotte could see that the thought was alien to Rachel. Family equaled love to the Connelly family.

"I know he doesn't. Why else would he never want to see me, never give me anything other than what would reflect well on him? Why else would he—"

"Okay," interrupted Rachel. "Enough. I can see this is important to you."

"It is. Rachel, what am I going to do?"

"Do? Why, that's the easiest part."

"It is?"

"Of course! All you need to do is get yourself a fiancé for the night. It shouldn't be that difficult. You're beautiful, accomplished, a real catch—you'll be fighting them off."

"Fighting who off?"

Rachel grabbed her phone and began searching for something. "The men who will reply to your dating ad."

Charlotte was appalled. "I'm not the kind of woman who needs to resort to a dating app!"

Rachel looked at her with a smile. "It would appear you're *exactly* the kind of woman who needs to use a dating app."

"No, I can't!"

Rachel sighed and put the phone down on the table. "Then the alternative is to find someone who would oblige."

She opened her mouth to speak but shut it again and shook her head.

Charlotte had a leap of hope. "What? Have you thought of someone?"

Rachel sucked her lips as she considered something. "I was thinking of my brothers."

"But they're married, except..." The last word disappeared into a sigh as Charlotte thought of a tall man of lean but wiry build with long curly blond hair and the face of an Adonis.

"Cam," finished Rachel. "He'd help, I'm sure."

"With all respect to your brother, Cameron isn't exactly the kind of man my father would approve of."

"Well, that's good, because he's not going to be posing as your *father's* fiancée."

Charlotte looked away. She couldn't meet Rachel's gaze. She knew what Rachel was saying, but she couldn't do anything about it. She'd spent her whole life trying to please her father and she couldn't seem to stop now, no matter what she did—which included moving thousands of miles away from Wellington to build a new life for herself in Akaroa. She knew she had to change, but knowing and truly believing seemed to be two different things.

"Cam would be great," continued Rachel. "He's the most intelligent person I know—excluding you."

"Brains don't equal smartness."

"They do in your case. But Cam? True, he can be a little... intense, and he does make some unusual decisions. And he's never on time. And you never really know what he's going to do next." Rachel sighed. "I guess he's kind of—"

"Quirky," interrupted Charlotte.

"I was going to say that maybe he's a little on the eccentric side. *Maybe*," she repeated, as if she felt guilty about accusing her brother of eccentricities.

"Maybe? You think? He's hopeless at conversation."

"He just doesn't like chit-chat. He only speaks if he's got something to say."

"Well, he doesn't often have something to say to me, that much is obvious!"

Rachel looked at her shrewdly. Charlotte's heart sank.

"You seem to be quite heated about my brother. In fact, you seem to have quite definite opinions about him. And yet I heard you called him, what was it, 'the most handsome man I've ever seen.'" Rachel smirked and Charlotte huffed indignantly.

"I *may* have said that, but what you're forgetting was that I'd had a few glasses of wine. It was at the end of Rob and Flo's wedding reception, and I was obviously feeling not quite myself."

"He *is* extremely handsome, in that English aesthetic way. Mum used to say he could have been a movie star."

Charlotte laughed. "I can't imagine your brother acting in any capacity."

"True. He's not like Dad, or me, come to that. How about it? I've seen the way he looks at you."

Charlotte blushed despite herself. "Like he wants to argue with me? Because that's all we seem to do on the few occasions we've met since Rob's wedding."

"No, like he wants to *ravish* you." Rachel laughed at Charlotte's expression. "Okay, okay." She glanced at her watch, then finished her drink and stood up. "Leave the whole date thing to me. I've got to go. Zane's picking me up."

"And I'm going to see Rob about this new case I've taken on."

"The Lake Waitahi case? Zane's told me a little about it. Hope you know what you're letting yourself in for," Rachel said, as she stood up and smoothed down her summer dress. Charlotte noticed every man had his eyes on Rachel who, even if she hadn't been well known through her TV cookery show, had the curvaceous figure which drew men's attention like moths to a flame. Not that Rachel noticed. She only had eyes for one man now, her husband, Zane.

Charlotte hoped Zane hadn't divulged all the details of the case to his wife. It was going to prove very contentious unless they all acted with discretion. But then Zane, as chair of the Ngai Tahu Tribal Council, was used to sensitive cases and was the model of integrity himself. Years before, he'd nearly lost Rachel by sticking to the letter of the law.

"I'm not sure I do. That's why I'm going to see Rob. Zane thought that, even if he couldn't help, he might know someone who could."

"True. Anyway," Rachel said. "Back to the important stuff. I'll set up your profile on a dating app and we'll go through them in a few days. See what we've netted."

Charlotte groaned.

"Charlotte! Do you want to tell the truth to your father or not?"

On that one point, Charlotte was clear. She shook her head. "Not."

"Then we will find you a man for the night."

"How bad does that sound?"

"It doesn't sound bad at all. *Fun* is what it sounds!" Rachel turned as Zane walked up to her, embraced her and kissed her deeply, as if they hadn't just seen each other only a few hours earlier.

Charlotte didn't groan again. Instead, she glanced away, farewelling them as she scooped up her phone and bag and walked toward the exit. It was one thing to find a man for an evening to look the part. It was quite another to be confronted with the thing she most wanted and, it seemed, couldn't ever get—the love of a good man.

I<small>T HAD BEEN</small> a long day of meetings and discussions which had progressively depressed Charlotte even further. Normally, she felt completely in control of any situation. But, as Rachel had foreseen, she was regretting having taken on this case where it seemed there was no middle ground, nowhere for her clients to come to a mutually acceptable agreement. As mediator in the dispute, finding such a compromise was key to a successful outcome. And the high-profile nature of the case could well either make or break her career. Not to mention impact on similar cases all around New Zealand. As she slammed the car door outside Flo's house, she couldn't help wondering if, for once, she'd taken on more than she could handle.

As soon as she opened the gate and two pairs of male eyes looked up at her from behind the garage where their owners were sitting, drinking beers, she knew she had. One pair of eyes belonged to Flo's father, Ian, who spent every weekend in the rooms and terrace which Rob had built onto the garage for him. The terrace looked more like an outdoor room, with its bright Tibetan prayer flags strung around the pergola, and furniture which lived permanently outside. It was here that he sat drinking beer with the other pair of male eyes—Cam's. The difference between them was that Cam's were focused on her with a laser-like focus. She could practically feel the prickle of heat on her skin as his unrelenting gaze followed her as she walked along the path to the house.

She waved and called out in acknowledgement of Flo's father's greeting, and gave Cam a quick, cool nod of the head. She quickened her pace, stumbling slightly on the uneven paving stones which led to Flo's front door which, apparently, only she used. It was open as usual. She glanced up at the newly constructed porch, perfectly in keeping with the rest of the colonial house. Despite the open door, she rang the bell.

Half-way along the hall, Flo popped her head out of the kitchen, wiping her hands on a towel. Charlotte didn't think she'd ever seen Flo's hands not busy. If they weren't floury, wet, or handling piles of linen, they had gardening gloves on or were holding a child's hand.

"Come in, Charlotte!" Flo called. "No need to stand on ceremony with us."

For a moment Charlotte saw herself as Flo saw her. As someone who always did things properly, someone who stood on ceremony, even, as she'd overheard once, as Miss Perfect. If only Flo knew the truth.

They exchanged small talk as Charlotte followed Flo into the kitchen where Flo was baking yet more cakes for Amber's café, besides the usual catering for her guests. Even after receiving enough money to do whatever she liked with her house and life, and marrying Rob Connelly, it seemed Flo refused to give up what she loved—nurturing people. And that included her stepson, Olly, who sat in the sunny window-seat ostensibly doing his homework, but really playing with a large white cat who flicked his tail, obviously irritated by the attention. Charlotte blinked. She was moving from one perfect family to the next. And they thought *she* was perfect! She'd do what she had to do and then leave—as soon as she could.

"Is Rob around?"

"Yes, he's expecting you. I think he's just gone out with the boys. I mean Dad and Cam. Those two have been inseparable since they've met. You go on outside if you like. Have you eaten?"

Had she? It took a few moments for Charlotte to realize

she hadn't eaten since breakfast and then it hadn't exactly been a feast.

"You haven't, have you?" said Flo reprovingly. "I'll bring something out to you."

"No, I'm fine thanks. Honestly." She was a little hungry but refused to be mothered by Flo. "But thank you," she said firmly, before stepping outside before Flo could remonstrate.

"Charlotte!" Rob said, appearing from inside Ian's rooms with a beer. He kissed her on the cheek while Ian jumped up and offered his chair next to Cam. "I'm glad you made it. I invited Cam to join us. I think he'll be able to help you out more than I will."

Charlotte looked askance at Cam. She knew he worked with plants, but, apart from that, knew little about what he did. She'd always made her excuses to leave whenever he was around. Cam's intense gaze hadn't shifted from her, and she could feel the heat rise in her cheeks as she forced herself to meet it.

"I get the feeling the very beautiful Charlotte Kincaid can't quite see what I can contribute to the problem with which she's confronted." He sipped his beer as he narrowed his eyes, which still held her gaze.

She cleared her throat, determined to ignore the fact that he'd just called her very beautiful. "Perhaps you could enlighten me," she said, refusing to lean back against the soft cushions. She sat up straight instead, her ankles crossed and her hands lightly clasped in front of her, desperately trying to adopt a professional attitude to defend herself from his charm.

"Sure." He smiled, as if realizing the cause of her discomfort and liking it. It was as if he knew exactly how much she was attracted to him. She felt humiliated that he should know this, but was determined to ignore it. "From what Rob tells me, you've been appointed mediator in the Lake Waitahi case. And you're an experienced mediator, so that must mean you're stuck between the rich and powerful farmers who are polluting the lake on one hand, and the Maori owners of the lake on the other."

"Correct." She looked around at the three men and decided to risk sharing a little more information with them. "The farmers refuse point blank to change their farming practices and the owners of the lake are going to lose money hand over fist as they fight to clean up the lake. I've been researching the subject, trying to figure out if there's some other means by which they could both get what they want. And then I read this article the other day about how planting could ease pollution problems and..." She hesitated, as she remembered the fizz of excitement she'd felt as she'd read the piece. Without thinking, she pressed her hand against her chest. "I don't know, I just felt that it might be the way forward."

For once, the aloof look on Cam's face had gone. He glanced at her hand, which was still pressed over her heart. Suddenly self-conscious, she lowered her hand. He looked into her eyes and they met with a connection which shot straight through the attraction and became something very different.

"You're passionate about it," said Cam.

She nodded, realizing for the first time that she was. This was different to any other case she'd mediated. She wanted to resolve the crisis, wanted to find an outcome that would be satisfactory for both parties but, at the moment, the only clue how she could do this had come with the article she'd read.

"Then I'll help you." He leaned back against the wooden bench, framed by the prayer flags. His handsome, sensitive features and intense gaze made him look as wise as she felt ignorant. "The article you mentioned, I was one of the peer reviewers for it." He waved his hand in a careless gesture. "It's my thing."

Rob grinned. "Talk about understatement of the year. What Cam *isn't* telling you, Charlotte, is that he's been working on the biodiversity of plants in marsh areas to reduce the impact of farming on waterways for years. He's your man."

Charlotte didn't know why Rob's last words struck her in such a personal way. She cleared her throat to rid herself of certain thoughts, which had been a feature of her daydreams ever since she'd first met Cam. Focus, Charlotte, focus.

"That, er, sounds exactly the expertise I need. Would you help us?"

"If I can do it before I leave, of course."

"When are you going?"

"In the New Year."

"Right." His imminent departure shouldn't have made her heart sink. "Well, at least we could get things started. Lay some groundwork. But I'm afraid the budget is limited."

"Even Charlotte has waived her fees for this job," said Rob.

"And so will I. Providing..."

Cam rested his arms on his legs and leaned toward Charlotte. She managed to stop herself from doing the same. He seemed to draw her to him like a magnet. She gritted her teeth and glanced at Rob and Ian, but they hadn't noticed and were busy talking about Flo and how she worked too hard. She turned back to Cam.

"Providing?" She held her breath, her imagination running riot with what kind of proviso Cam would come up with.

"Providing I get to call you Charlie." He leaned back against the cushioned chair with a grin, lifted one foot onto the opposite knee and took a swig from his beer bottle.

Charlotte's smile faded instantly. "Charlie isn't my name. Charlotte is."

"You need to loosen up, if you don't mind me saying."

"I do mind," she said, picking up her bag. She wasn't going to sit around and be made fun of.

"And I reckon me calling you Charlie will be good," continued Cam, as if he hadn't been interrupted by her denial.

She rose with a tight smile. "Good for you or me?"

"Both, maybe," he said in that low, sexy voice which never hurried. Cam wasn't a conversationalist like his brother, Gabe, but when he spoke everyone stopped talking and listened to him, such was his magnetism. "If you play your cards right."

"I don't play cards," she said primly, clutching her bag in front of her as if it would defend her from Cam's flirtation. She stepped away, desperate to be outside Cam's compelling orbit. "Anyway, I have to go now." She paused as she remembered she needed him more than he needed her. "Perhaps we could discuss the matter tomorrow, to educate me on all the relevant facts."

"Sure thing," said Cam. He rose in an odd, old-fashioned, gentlemanly manner and, whether or not she wanted him to, joined her as she walked to the garden gate. He opened it for her and stepped aside. "I look forward to educating you tomorrow."

"Sure, thanks," she said, hurrying out the gate and almost running toward the car. It took her two goes to unlock the car door and then she jumped in and took off like a bat out of hell, without a backward glance.

Never in her life had she been so challenged, placed so out of her depth by a person. Not her father, not any friends or lovers. But this man, who'd turned up on Flo's doorstep the night of Flo and Rob's wedding, looking like a movie-star playing a drifter, had done just that. She had to make sure it wouldn't happen again. If she had to make a list about why not, she'd have said (1) he was the opposite of everything she'd always wanted in a man, apart from his good looks and (2) he was leaving in a few weeks' time. And both spelled danger. On that point, she needed no education.

2

The next day, after any number of meditations, yoga and good old-fashioned talking-tos, Charlotte felt more herself, more in control again. Unfortunately, that feeling was dented somewhat when Rachel suggested they catch up at Belendroit to go over the responses to the dating app. And, after that, she'd arranged to give Cam a lift to Lake Waitahi.

Belendroit. She'd never been to the property. In fact, she'd avoided going there, and didn't relish the prospect now. She knew some members of the Connelly family well—especially Rachel and Rob—and they talked about the place as if it meant more to them than a house in which they'd been raised. Instinctively, she'd avoided the place, evading all invitations, until now. But she still couldn't miss seeing the place from Akaroa. Especially at night, when the dark trees around the homestead twinkled with the lanterns after which the bay was named.

She knew why she'd been avoiding the place. It represented everything she wanted and everything she had no hope of getting if the past few years were anything to go by.

The men she was attracted to were all after one thing—*not* marriage, and *definitely* not children. She wanted both, and she wanted them with the man of her dreams. All she had to do was find him. In the meantime, it looked like she'd have to toughen up and see Belendroit in person, because Rachel was busy filming and Cam apparently didn't, or wouldn't, drive.

Wonderful, she thought, as she drove out of Akaroa. At least she'd made sure Cam wouldn't be arriving at Belendroit until 2pm. That gave her half-an-hour to sort the blind dates out. She felt a little queasy at the thought of it, but this was for her father. Her father, Christmas, and a fictitious fiancé. How hard could it be? She wiped away a prickle of sweat from her forehead.

She turned off the road and drove along a drive through a small copse of trees strung with lanterns, before emerging into a sunny clearing, in the middle of which stood the house. Flowers bloomed everywhere. From the towering blue and purple foxgloves and lupins to the wildflowers, which created a shifting haze of color—orange, blue, yellow —amongst the trees, the garden was a mass of color. White clematis grew up on one side of the house and around a lantern. And, on the other side, threading their way through the wisteria, out of control, flame-colored nasturtiums created a vivid contrast to the vibrant blue of the sea. She parked, ducked her head down to look at the house through the windscreen, and gave a low whistle. Charlotte wasn't sure what she'd expected, but it certainly wasn't this.

She'd seen the house from Akaroa, peeping out from the trees, but she'd never been along the road which led to it. Few people drove in that direction, as it became unsealed shortly after Belendroit and only led to the end of the peninsular, some miles distant. To say it was a house with character was an understatement. It looked like it was smiling in surprise. She had to admit that, with the trees framing it, and the summer flowers in bloom, it had to be the most welcoming house she'd ever seen. It wasn't anything like she'd expected. It unnerved her.

And it took a lot to unnerve her. Most things didn't. Most things demanded nothing of her. High-end elegance didn't faze her. She'd heard what Amber and Flo thought of St Augustine's—a restaurant in the hills to which anyone who could pay the prices came from miles around—but such things didn't bother her. And grinding poverty and unpredictability didn't faze her. She helped at the Christchurch City Mission, both as a lawyer and a volunteer. Neither sides of life affected her. But this place did. She swallowed down the flutter of nerves, got out of the car and quietly closed the door. It didn't seem the place to slam a car door. The atmosphere was gentle and enveloping and instantly soothed her nerves.

As she approached, the illusion of the smiling house broke a little as she realized it was the way the veranda fretwork framed the door which gave the house its smile. And the raised eyebrows were only the roof jutting out over the first-floor dormer windows. Just an illusion, she said to herself firmly. Nothing more. But still she couldn't shed the feeling of peace which entered her and refused to leave.

She continued walking between the two wings of the house and up the steps towards the open front door, beside which a wide veranda provided welcome shade from the sun. She hesitated in front of the door as she heard voices above the sound of jazz music. She held her breath to listen for a response. Surely Cam wouldn't have arrived so early?

She walked up the steps, knocked on the door, and looked into the hallway. It was wide, with high ceilings, and filled with the clutter of generations. The wide-planked polished floorboards were covered with rugs and appeared to lead towards the kitchen, which sat at the heart of the house.

"Hello?" she called, not wanting to enter the house. She didn't do that kind of thing. "Rachel? Cameron? Jim?" Then she heard a clatter of pans and Jim Connelly emerged from the kitchen at the far end of the hall.

"Charlotte! How lovely to see you," he said, as he went to kiss her, thought better of it, and shook her hand instead.

"Jim," she said, relieved to have been spared one of his big hugs. "How are you?"

"Can't complain!"

"Good. Is Cameron here?" She had to ask, because there was no way she'd be talking with Rachel about her dates if he was.

"No! Haven't seen him since he went out for a walk hours ago. But then I've been in the kitchen with Rachel and her camera crew. Such fun," he said, with a wide smile.

Charlotte thought Rachel was correct—that Jim enjoyed her using Belendroit's kitchen for her TV cookery series, even more than she did.

"Ah, good."

He frowned. "Should he be here?"

"Not yet. We agreed I'd pick him up from here at two."

"Come in, come in," said Jim. "We don't stand on ceremony here. Rachel will be free in a minute. She's just talking with the crew out the back of the house."

She found herself ushered into the kitchen. Of course, she knew what the kitchen looked like since Rachel had started using it for her cooking programmes, but was still struck by the grandeur of its proportions and the blend of homely touches which only old kitchen paraphernalia could bring, along with Rachel's own line of crockery and kitchen utensils, many of which hung from the overhead hanging basket.

"This is even more charming than it appears on the TV."

Jim filled the kettle and placed it on its stand. "Yes, I suppose it is. It's been in the family for generations, and my late wife added to the charm with layers of her own. And my daughters—especially Rachel—have added yet more to it." Charlotte followed his gaze around the room as it settled first on a group of watercolor paintings of Belendroit, and then the overhead wire hanger from which every conceivable kitchen utensil hung. He nodded toward it. "At least Rachel stopped her set designers from replacing all the old family stuff. There are things in there that should be in a museum."

"No, Dad," said Rachel, stepping into the kitchen with a big smile. "They belong in a home. Museums are for dead things, and Belendroit is very much alive." She kissed Charlotte on both cheeks before giving Jim a hug for good measure.

Jim's face settled into soft wrinkles as he smiled warmly at his daughter, before putting his arm around her and kissing her cheek. Charlotte swallowed and looked away. She'd never seen such warmth and affection in her father. But it looked like Rachel was used to it, and continued making the tea as if nothing unusual had happened. Such love and such ease. It stung at the heart of her.

"Let's chat outside, shall we? I've been filming inside all day and am dying to be in the fresh air on such a glorious day. Are you coming, Dad?"

"No, you girls go and chat. I'm feeling a bit jaded. All this excitement," he added with a forced smile. Rachel frowned. "Are you okay, Dad?"

"Of course, of course. Just a bit tired. You girls go without me." He shooed them out the door.

"Okay, if you're sure. Let's sit outside"—Rachel brandished her iPad—"and check through to see what we've netted."

Charlotte groaned and sat down where Rachel indicated. She looked around, but there was no sign of anyone. There were a few windows open and she could hear activity coming from the other end of the house. But she still felt the uneasy sensation that they might be overheard.

"Are you sure no one else is around? I'd be mortified if anyone else knew what we were doing."

"Of course not! They're all at work, anyway."

"Cameron?" asked Charlotte quietly, knowing that he wasn't working on his brief stay in New Zealand.

Rachel waved her hand. "He went out this morning. I told him you'd pick him up from here at two, and he's always late. I don't know why my brother avoids driving cars unless he absolutely has to. Some ecological reason, no doubt."

"But you're sure he's not here?"

"The only member of my family I've seen these last few hours is my father, who is now well out of earshot and is lying down in his bedroom." Rachel stretched out her hand and squeezed Charlotte's. "Don't worry. Anyway, aren't you excited to see who's responded to your profile?"

"I guess. Although I haven't actually *seen* my profile yet."

Rachel swept her fingers over the iPad. "Here." She turned the screen to Charlotte. "High-powered lawyer wanting a professional man for date. Interested in conversation, friendship and fun."

Charlotte frowned at the last word. "Fun?" she repeated faintly.

"Fun," said Rachel firmly. "I know you only said 'conversation and friendship', but I thought that sounded a little dull."

"Maybe I *am* a little dull."

"You're not at all dull. Anyway," continued Rachel, "what do you think of this lot?" She handed the iPad to Charlotte.

Charlotte gave a low whistle. "That's a lot of men!" She

widened her eyes at some of the photos which revealed buff, handsome men with appealing smiles, winced at some others, and squeaked at a few other photos which could only be described as sleazy, and which were met with a swift left swipe. Then she began again, propping up the iPad between them so they could both see.

"Okay, the second run through, I'll check out what they say."

"What they say?" asked Rachel, giving her an odd look. "Not how they look?"

"No. The first run through was to de-sleaze, and the second is to assess their resumé."

"Resumé? It's not a job interview!"

"You're wrong. It most certainly *is* a job interview." Charlotte flicked through pages, swiping right or left with instant decision.

"What was wrong with him?"

"Can't spell," said Charlotte. She tutted. "And this one likes skinny dipping. Ugh."

"What's wrong with skinny dipping? Amber does it all the time."

"Well, as lovely as Amber is, I have no wish to date her either." Charlotte paused on another photo. "Nor do I wish to date someone with muscles like that."

"So he goes to the gym. You *surely* can't be against that?"

"What I'm against is someone who enjoys showing them off like that. I mean, that pose. It's, it's…"

Rachel peered closer. "It's incredibly sexy, is what it is."

Charlotte shot her friend a disapproving look and nudged the iPad back into position. "And that's not what I want. Can you imagine my father discussing politics with someone like that?"

Charlotte could feel Rachel's incredulous gaze turn to her. "I guess you don't mean the leftist politics that a"—she frowned as she read the text—"union organizer might have."

"Certainly not. My father is definitely at the other end of the spectrum. Far right of right, I guess you could say."

Rachel sat back and took a sip of her tea. "This is trickier than I imagined. I think I'll leave it to you."

It was easier without Rachel looking over her shoulder. Charlotte didn't have to justify why, on her third run through, she'd ditched the most handsome of the men—she didn't trust handsome. In her experience, good-looking men were always more interested in themselves than anybody else. Within minutes, she had her top three. She passed the iPad to Rachel.

"Here are the top three candidates." She pointed at one. "That one will do."

Rachel shook her head and tapped the screen as she arranged the date. She sat back with a sigh and folded her arms.

"What?" asked Charlotte.

"I thought this was going to be fun. You know, us, drooling over the men, laughing over others, figuring out any coded meaning in their bios."

"There is nothing fun about making such an important choice."

"So it seems," said Rachel, snapping shut the iPad. She tapped her fingernails against its case for a few moments. "You know, Charlotte, I think you're taking this all a bit seriously. I mean, your father is coming to see *you* at Christmas."

"No, you're wrong. My father is coming to see if I measure up to his ideals, to meet the fiancé who doesn't exist, and to pass judgement on my lifestyle. He's a High Court Judge, remember."

"Oh." Rachel squeezed Charlotte's arm in a show of sympathy. In the past, Charlotte had always done her utmost to avoid people touching her, but Rachel Connelly and—it was becoming clear—her siblings were people she didn't have the heart to rebuff. She felt some of the fight drain out of her. "That sounds grim."

"It *is* grim. That's why I left to make a fresh start for myself here. I couldn't escape my father's influence in Wellington—it was too small. Coming here has been a revelation. It's the first time I feel I've had a real life of my own."

"If you want a real life," said Rachel, "then maybe you need something more than to simply move from one place to another."

"Like?"

"Get yourself a new attitude."

Charlotte looked away with a frown.

"Starting here," Rachel continued. "You've discarded some of these men on the flimsiest of reasons. It looks to me as if you're scared to loosen control over your life. But, you know, if you meet the right man, it won't feel like that."

Charlotte pretended to rummage in her bag for her car keys. She didn't want Rachel to see how her words had affected her. She hooked out the keys. "Here they are!" she said too brightly.

But Rachel wasn't easily fooled. "Charlotte," she said in a warning tone.

Charlotte sighed, looking away. "It's easy for you to say. You've met the right man."

"Believe me," said Rachel, dipping her head until Charlotte was forced to meet her sympathetic gaze, "I had to go through a lot of anguish before I found Zane. And, even then, it was hard. Probably the hardest thing I've done in my life. But we got there. And so will you."

Rachel had told Charlotte about her past, and she suddenly felt contrite that she was bemoaning her own fate when Rachel had been through so much.

"I hope I even have a fraction of what you have—a loving husband, children and extended family. You are blessed, Rachel."

"And so will you be." Rachel glanced at the iPad. "Especially if you leave your pre-conceived ideas behind and go with the fun guys."

Charlotte was about to remonstrate once more when she heard someone cough—the kind of artificial cough you made when you wanted to draw attention to yourself. They both turned sharply to see Cam, arms propped on the open window, looking at them, amusement sparkling in his eyes.

"If you're done sorting out your love life—over which I agree with Rachel in case you're interested—perhaps we should get going. It's past two."

"What the hell are you doing here, Cam?" shouted Rachel in a strangled voice, looking across at Charlotte with a concerned expression. "Were you eavesdropping?" she asked, turning back to Cam.

Cam looked as cool and handsome as ever, his blond hair swept back off his face, revealing a perfect bone structure and eyes which never missed a thing.

"I was listening to music on the headphones while you were filming in the kitchen. And then the music stopped"—he grinned—"and the entertainment began."

Rachel grunted in frustration and threw one of the dogs' toys at Cam, who, frustratingly, caught it. "You are impossible, Cam. *Impossible*. We were talking privately here." She grimaced ruefully at Charlotte. "I'm so sorry, Charlotte. I thought we were alone."

Charlotte turned her beetroot face away, dying inside as she re-ran her conversation with Rachel in her mind, going over what they'd said and what Cam might have heard. Take a minute, she said to herself, as she collected her things. Just a minute. It was always what she'd done when things had been desperate at home, or at work, or in her personal life. Take a minute, breathe and wait for the emotions to clear, because life was a lot easier without emotions. Her parents had shown her that.

"It's okay," she eventually said. "We were simply doing some business. Nothing more." Ignoring the blush which refused to leave her cheeks, she forced herself to look at Cam, whose smile fell as their gazes met. "And Cameron is right, it's time to go." Her smile, too, was forced when she turned to Rachel. "Thanks for everything. I'll catch up with you later."

Whatever had happened, Charlotte knew Rachel was entirely innocent. Rachel had been convinced no one was around. No, Charlotte thought as she hurried down the steps toward the car. The only person responsible for her humiliation was Cam.

CAM WASN'T sure if he was more surprised by the exceedingly lovely Charlotte Kincaid using a dating app— why would she have to?—or the wonderful blush of embarrassment which filled her usually fair and perfect complexion. Her lips were tight and her eyes bright and darting. His fascination with this woman had just stepped up a notch.

She'd already begun revving the car when he jumped into the passenger seat. Her confusion ruffled that perfect exterior, revealing more of herself than she usually allowed to be seen. She refused to return his gaze and drove too quickly along the drive, bumping over some new potholes which had appeared in the drive, forcing him to grip the door handle to steady himself.

"I hope your dating isn't as rough as your driving," he commented.

"My dating," she said, emphasizing each syllable, "isn't any of your business."

"Maybe not, but getting us both to Lake Waitahi in one piece is," he said pointedly, as she crunched the gears upon entering the road. Her lips formed an even firmer line as she increased speed along the road toward Akaroa. He sighed and settled back for an uncomfortable journey. If she wanted silence, then so be it.

"Did you check through the information I emailed you last night?" she eventually asked.

He raised an eyebrow at her. "My homework, you mean?"

She nodded curtly.

"Sure."

He knew she was waiting for him to expand, but he couldn't be bothered. He wound down his window and waved at Amber, who was outside her café, chatting to her customers. She waved back and called out a greeting.

"She's such a sweet kid," he said, raising his window again.

"Kid? She owns the café, is a respected artist, and is married and expecting twins."

"She's still my kid sister to me."

She grunted.

He was intrigued. "And what does that dismissive grunt mean?"

She gave a tight shrug. She obviously still hadn't recovered from the knowledge that he'd overheard her dating plans. He'd leave it for now but, when the time was right, he fully intended to pick up that thread with her.

"Just that you underestimate her."

She was trying to annoy him, but she had yet to learn that he rarely got annoyed. He didn't attempt to suppress a smile. "No, I don't."

"Yes, you do." Her grip tightened on the steering wheel,

and her immaculately manicured nails tapped lightly on the leather. "You don't rate anyone who's different from you."

His good humor faltered slightly. "Where do you get that idea?"

She shot him a sharp glance. "You. You coolly watch everyone, judging them all the while. I doubt anyone ever reaches the dizzying heights of your standards."

This was getting interesting, and he hadn't even brought up the blind dates yet. "You're wrong. I don't judge people. I'm interested in them, sure, but you've mistaken my interest for judgement. I accept people for who they are."

She blinked twice and then bit her lip as she focused on the twists and turns of the road as they ascended the range of hills which enclosed Akaroa Harbor. Something he'd said had taken her from ruffled to upset. He didn't like that.

"Is there something wrong with accepting people for who they are?" he asked more gently now, wanting the distress in her eyes to disappear.

She shrugged. "No. It's just something I'm not used to."

"Ah, Rachel mentioned your father is a High Court Judge. Perhaps that's why you assume I judge everyone."

She shot him another look, obviously perturbed to think she'd been the subject of their conversation.

"We weren't gossiping about you, if that's what you're thinking. I asked Rachel if you were coming to Belendroit for Christmas." Her eyes widened, but it could have been the hairpin bend. "But she said your father was visiting, so she doubted it."

"He's arriving Christmas Eve."

"That's nice. It's good to be with family. I'd almost forgotten how good."

He noticed her shoulders relax a little. He was on the right track.

"It's the first time he's been down here. I invite him every Christmas."

"And he lives in Wellington? That's only an hour's flight away."

She nodded, and his heart sank as her usually beautiful lips re-formed a grim line. "He's a busy man."

Suddenly, it clicked. "Right. So I'm guessing it's no coincidence that you're hunting around for a date on Christmas Eve when he's going to visit you?"

Her hands twisted around the steering wheel. Any tighter and she'd wrench the thing off. "We'll be at the lake in twenty minutes, so I suggest we talk business. There are a lot more important things at stake here than my personal life."

"More important, maybe, but not half as interesting." He grinned, but she didn't.

"The stakes, Cameron."

"The stakes, Charlie."

She sucked in a deep breath through gritted teeth before continuing to talk about the project he'd agreed to help her with. He knew it all already, but let her talk. He enjoyed listening to her analytical brain in action. She was smart. And she was also smart enough to know the limits of her expertise, which was uncommonly smart. He waited until she finished talking.

"So," he said, summing up. "We have an amazing lake of significance to local Maori, being polluted by wealthy and powerful farmers from the surrounding land who have no desire, or incentive, to change their ways. It's all legal and above board and there's nothing the Maori owners can do to stop it."

"That about sums it up."

"Except you. You've taken on the job of mediating between them."

"Zane recommended me. He's part of the tribe who owns the lake."

"Zane must hold you in high esteem to suggest you take on such a strategically important job as this. A job which could have implications for the whole of New Zealand."

"Yes, but I'm afraid I'll let him down. I can't seem to find a point of agreement, anywhere at all, from which to work. That was until I read the article I told you about which led me to the Swedish Wetlands project."

"You won't let him down because I set up the Swedish project, and have a good idea how we can improve the water quality of the lake by using a comparatively small investment which we will guilt the farmers to fund. You wanted a win-win, and I reckon you've found one."

Charlotte gave a relieved sigh. "I hope so."

He twisted around to face her, looping his arm over the back of the car seat. "Between Zane with your work, and Rachel with your love-life, I reckon that power couple have you covered. Now, tell me, what do you do for fun?"

"I enjoy everything I do," she said. "What do *you* do for fun?" she countered.

He was enjoying this. It was like an evenly matched game of table tennis. He'd just lobbed a ball over the net and she'd neatly returned it.

"Oh, the usual. Work—you can't beat working with nature, outside, improving things for generations to come. My mother taught me that. And play."

"Play?" she probed, continuing the volley of words.

"The usual. Exercise—I run. And sex."

Ha! He returned the loose ball with a smash and sat back to watch her reaction.

She blushed again, her eyes widening and brightening with shocked embarrassment. He could imagine the same bright eyes looking into his, the same gasp, as he made love to her—something he'd imagined doing from the very first time they'd met after Rob and Flo's wedding. The attraction had been instant and had only grown each time they'd met since.

"Don't get me wrong," he murmured, noting the husky tone which had crept into his voice, "I'm not keen on casual sex. For me, sex has to have meaning, has to be with the mind and the body." His hand was already close to her hair. A long strand had escaped her French twist and he couldn't resist extending his fingers and brushing them over it. It was as silky as it looked.

"Don't do that!" she snapped.

"Sorry," he said, withdrawing his hand. "I couldn't resist."

"If you think all this talk about sex is going to get me into your bed, you've another think coming!"

"I think you protest too much. Come on, Charlie, you can't deny the connection we have. I see it in your eyes and I feel it here." He pressed his hand against his gut. "My sacral chakra, gut reaction. Call it what you will, but it rules my life and you should let it rule yours."

"My *mind* rules my life, not my stomach. You're talking nonsense, Cam. There is no place in my life for chaos, and that is what you are. Chaos with a capital C."

"It looks like Cam with a capital C and Chaos with a capital C go together. How about Charlie with a capital C, too? But, seriously, chaos can be fun. You should try it sometime. In fact, while I think about it, why don't *I* be your date for Christmas Eve? I can discuss politics with your father."

"Ha! You're as left-wing as they come and my father is as right-wing as they come."

"Then it'll be an interesting discussion and we'll have plenty to talk about. Or we can talk philosophy."

"Like what?" she asked dismissively.

"Like... the ethical concept of Consequentialism, for

example. I'm sure we could have a lively debate about that," he said with a grin. "It *is* a thing, you know—about the ethics of judging people according to the consequences of their actions."

"I *know* it's a thing," she said between gritted teeth. "I studied it."

"I'm sure it will be an entertaining discussion."

"That's irrelevant, because there will be no such discussion. Because Cameron, you're not coming within a one-mile radius of my father. You're the total opposite to him, and the total opposite to me."

"You're wrong, again," he said, checking their location as they approached the lake.

"Then it seems you don't know me as well as you imagine you do," she said, stopping the car with a jolt, as her foot slammed, with unnecessary force, onto the brake. "I'm never wrong."

He watched her get out of the car and greet a couple of people who were waiting for them. He knew he wasn't wrong. He knew from the little fissures which had appeared in Miss Charlotte Kincaid's—or Miss Perfect, as he'd heard Flo call her—facade that Charlotte was a woman who had hidden her emotional self so deeply that even she didn't know it existed.

He'd always liked a challenge.

---

3

*I*t was taking Charlotte much longer than it should have to regain her usual feeling of calm, which sitting so close to Cam Connelly had destroyed. Even after they'd joined the others for the meeting and there was no chance for him to talk about the personal, she still felt unsettled. Watching him take control of the meeting and talk with such passion and knowledge about the lake, and how it and the surrounding land could be improved, had impressed both the representatives of the Maori tribe who owned the lake and her.

Now, as they walked along the lake edge and Cam showed the group how it could look with the pair of virtual reality goggles which, unbeknownst to her, he'd had in his unprepossessing rucksack, even her discomfort had been replaced by awe.

She was used to handling complex legal arguments and a wide variety of people, but Cam had her beat on both counts. He had a natural empathy for people, usually hidden by his aloofness, and a brain which somehow combined complex scientific data with an appreciation of the *wairua* of a place—its spirit. What had at first appeared to be a chaotic mix of ideas and beliefs seemed to sit easily with him. Somehow they formed a complete approach to life and people, which had her baffled. She'd underestimated him.

By the end of the meeting the lake owners had agreed on the approach which she and Cam had proposed—fight the pollution with planting and structural changes around the lake and fund it out of the pockets of the farmers who would be grateful to have their livelihoods and image saved.

It was late by the time she and Cam began the drive back to Akaroa. Cam was invigorated. She felt exhausted, not least by the internal struggle of both admiring Cam and fearing his impact on her peace of mind—and body. More talkative than on the drive to the lake, it seemed he was inspired by the attitude of the Maori owners, which was far more progressive than some people he'd been working with on similar projects in Europe.

"You're quiet," he said, after twisting in his seat and looking at her for a while.

"I'm driving," she said.

"I thought you women could all multi-task—drive *and* talk."

"You've mistaken me for 'all women,'" she said dryly.

"You're not like any woman I know, Charlie."

She winced at his use of her nickname, which no one else had ever used, while at the same time feeling impossibly flattered that he thought her to be different. She could tell by his tone that she was different in a good way. "Charlotte," she corrected half-heartedly, unwilling to acknowledge his compliment.

He sighed as he realized she would not acknowledge his comment, and leaned back against the car seat, his head tilted to hers. "You look like a Charlie to me."

She shot him a quick glance before focusing once more on the road. "Cute and girlie? I don't think so."

"Nor do I. But I reckon Charlotte is too formal, too one-dimensional—it doesn't sum up the real you."

"And you think you know the real me, do you?"

"I wouldn't be so arrogant."

She shot him a disbelieving look, before concentrating on the road as it began the steep and winding ascent of the hills which separated the lake from Akaroa.

He grinned. "You think me arrogant, too?"

"Yes," she said, overtaking a truck, which had pulled over into the slow lane, with a friendly beep of the horn.

"Yes, I guess you're probably right. I don't believe there's any place for false modesty in this world. Waste of time. I know what I'm like."

"And like what you know, no doubt," she said, with a despairing sigh. This man was like a fascinating puzzle—he got under her skin emotionally, challenged her brain intellectually, until she couldn't seem to rid herself of him. If she didn't watch out, he'd become an obsession. *That* would be a first.

His grin widened. "Of course. I'm not into hating myself. Although, you now, I bet *you* don't like *your*self."

She gripped the steering wheel more tightly. "Now why wouldn't I like myself?"

"That's what I'm curious about. Take your father, for instance. What on earth would induce you to create a pretend fiancé to tempt your father to visit you, which, I understand, he has never done?"

She opened her mouth to speak, but shook her head instead and clamped her lips down. She refused to answer such a personal question.

But he leaned in closer to her, until she could swear she could feel the warmth of his breath on her neck, prickling her skin and sending darting shivers down her spine before they coalesced and nestled deep inside of her, stirring her like she'd never been stirred before.

"Poor only child of a broken home…" he murmured. "Needing love and attention and never getting it, no matter how hard she tried."

The stirrings stopped abruptly, overcome by the pain of someone stamping on her fears and insecurities—of someone understanding her too well.

She licked her lips. "If what you say *wasn't* true, it would be mean. If what you say *was* true, it would be even meaner. I didn't take you for a cruel person, Cameron." Her reply was softly spoken—it was all she could manage—but he sat back in his seat as if he she'd slapped him.

"I'm sorry," he eventually said. "I didn't intend to be cruel, only to shake you up a bit. To get under your skin. But I guess sometimes uncovering the truth hurts. Especially if that truth has been covered so well for a long time and gone unacknowledged."

She blinked as she considered his words. They were approaching Akaroa now, and she slowed as she entered the village. She could keep silent, but she, like Cam, had always prided herself on facing the truth. And she had done so in every aspect of her life except, perhaps, where it mattered most—with herself.

"You're right. I wish you weren't."

"You don't need your father's approbation, Charlie. You're enough—*more* than enough—without it. You are an amazing woman and if your father can't see that, can't love you because of it, or without it, then I reckon you're best off without him."

She slowed to a crawl as they were forced to stop behind a van which was blocking the road. They watched the van driver unload, and she returned the man's wave. She didn't speak immediately. She needed those moments to recover from the fact that Cam appeared to find her amazing. "It's one thing to think that, Cameron, quite another to truly believe it." She turned off the engine and tapped her heart. "In here."

His expression softened more than she'd ever seen before. He took her hand from her heart and brought it to his lips, kissing it so tenderly that it almost broke her heart. She tried hard, but failed to suppress a small gasp.

"Emotions will be the death of us, won't they, Charlie? We're kindred spirits, you and I—letting our minds rule our hearts and lives."

She glanced at him, touched by his directness and honesty. She had been trying to block out her emotions all her life, as if they were like some kind of Chernobyl explosion waiting to happen. She'd encased them in mental concrete, but still they wouldn't die. Just kept on chugging out the heat and confusion, twisting things into different shapes as they tried to escape. Her emotions around her father were certainly curiously childish. She knew this, but still didn't seem able to stop them.

"I..." She hesitated. She'd never spoken of her emotions, her feelings for her family, of her hopes for the future to anyone, not even to Rachel. And yet here was Rachel's brother, Cam, the person who most aggravated her and most attracted her, making a connection no one else had. "I guess there's something in what you say."

"Yes, there's something, and if you can't see it, then you're never going to be free of it." He paused. "Why don't you come and have a drink with me now? We can talk."

She opened her mouth to say the only word she wanted to say—'yes'—to his suggestion, but she suddenly remembered that she had the first of her blind dates arranged for that evening.

"I can't. I have plans."

"Cancel them."

"I can't."

"You can't always work."

"It's not work. It's a date."

He huffed in disbelief and shook his head. "Not one of your blind dates?"

She nodded, unable to say the words out loud. What on earth had possessed her to agree to Rachel's suggestion? But she knew. It was exactly as Cam had said. She was desperate to please her father, desperate to have him approve of her, to love her. Emotionally, she hadn't progressed from a child, and she hated it.

"Then why don't you drop me off here? I can walk the rest of the way." He opened the car door and stepped out onto the pavement, exchanging a few friendly words with the van driver, who was now pulling away. Before he closed the door, he dipped his head and looked at her for a few thoughtful moments. "Thanks for the lift."

The car door slammed, and she drove off feeling ridiculous, humiliated and angry all at once. What was it to Cam, whether she went on a date? He'd made it clear to everyone that he was leaving as soon as Christmas was over, no matter how 'amazing' he found her. Come New Year, he'd be gone, so what was the point of going out for a drink—as a friend or a date? And she hadn't a clue which one he was meaning.

CAM TOOK a swig of his beer and looked morosely around the crowded pub. It was much smarter than when he'd used to come here as a boy, darting in when the bar manager wasn't looking and sneaking a sip of his uncle's beer.

Gabe, his younger brother, punched him in the arm. "Hey, what's up? It's not like you to be miserable."

"How would you know? I've been absent for years."

"True," said Gabe, unperturbed. Sometimes Gabe completely baffled him by his good nature, which had become even sunnier since he'd married the tall, blonde and gorgeous Maddy. "But there's only one thing I know of which makes people so down."

"Oh yeah? War, famine, death, disaster, that kind of thing?"

"Nope," said Gabe, finishing his beer. "Women."

"Women," repeated Cam, adding an edge to the word.

"Yep. And I'm a doctor, so I know what I'm talking about."

Cam couldn't help returning Gabe's grin. It was impossible to feel grumpy around him. He and Amber were the sunniest of the Connelly clan and always lit up whatever room they were in. When they were together—which was most lunchtimes in Amber's café—the wattage was brilliant, casting a halo over everything. They were everything he wasn't and, not for the first time, he felt a flash of envy at how easily he imagined their lives were because of it.

Gabe stood up and pointed to Cam's beer. "Want another one of those?"

"No, I'm off."

"Home?"

"Belendroit," he said firmly. He refused to think of the place in which he'd been raised as home. He didn't need a home. He simply lived his life wherever he was. The thought that he avoided Belendroit pressed at his mind, but he refused to analyze it. What he'd said to Charlotte was true. Emotions would be the death of him and he refused to do more than acknowledge the effect being at Belendroit had on him. "Yes, I thought I'd go for a wander around the streets first. A trip down memory lane."

"It doesn't have to be only in the memory, you know. It can be in the present too."

Cam knew exactly what Gabe was saying. "For you, maybe, but not me. That's not what I do."

"It's what you *could* do. Stay. It would make a change. You might find you like it."

Cam muttered an expletive, and Gabe grinned. What did it take to make Gabe angry? Amber had told him what it took to upset Gabe—nearly losing Maddy—but anger? Cam thought the world would end before his brother lost his temper.

"You've been a doctor for too long. I don't need curing. I'm perfectly well."

"Well, maybe. But happy? I'm not so sure. You live too much in your head."

Cam jumped up. "Enough of the analysis already. I'm off. I'll see you later." He took a few paces, turned back and grinned. "Give Maddy a kiss from me." Gabe scowled, and Cam laughed. At last he'd got a rise out of him. As he walked outside into the cool evening air, he contemplated his sister-in-law. She was beautiful, slightly aloof until you got to know her—which he still hadn't really—and accomplished. Just like most of the other women he knew who were also attractive, with all the things he enjoyed—interesting, good conversation, sexy, especially sexy—he felt little desire for them other than the obvious. Which begged the question—who was his sort of woman?

This was where his mind failed him, and some other elusive combination of spirit, heart and mind joined forces and placed a damned big magnet between him and Charlotte. She was exasperating. She had control so nailed down it wasn't funny, and her emotions around her father revealed a heart that was hurting. And he couldn't stop thinking about her when he wasn't with her. And, when he *was* with her, he couldn't stop teasing her, or trying to ruffle that armor-plated shield to reveal the real her. Because, as much as the image Charlotte projected to the world attracted him, it was the glimpse of the woman hiding behind that image which intrigued him. He instinctively knew that the real woman would be magic.

Which brought him back to the real reason he was wandering the streets of Akaroa. He'd accidentally over-heard Rachel telling Amber where Charlotte was meeting her date and thought a night cap might be just the thing. Just to make sure she was okay. That was all. But, as he crossed the road to enter the bar, he saw something which made him stop in his tracks. Charlotte was in a window seat with her date. He watched as she jumped up and spoke in a way which her body language made clear was angry. He backed into the shadows. It looked like he wouldn't have to break up the date, because it appeared Charlotte was doing exactly that. Still, he'd wait, just to make sure she was safe.

"WHAT DON'T you understand about 'no'?" asked Charlotte, exasperated, as she jumped up and collected the bill. No way would she let this jerk pay for her meal. He already seemed to think she owed him something.

"I don't understand 'no' at all." Her date grinned and rose, stretching ostentatiously in his tight black t-shirt, as if wanting to show off the muscles to all the world. She shouldn't have listened to Rachel about muscles. Charlotte had been correct—they simply showed a person was self-obsessed. "To me, all 'no' means is a challenge."

Charlotte was done talking with her date. There was no way she could get through to him. Instead, she stalked over to the desk and handed over her credit card, tapping her fingers agitatedly, hoping he wouldn't catch her up. But she turned around to find he'd followed her.

"Hey, beautiful, where are you off to in such a hurry?"

"I have to go," said Charlotte, stuffing her credit card back into her purse. "Goodnight."

But instead of taking the hint, he slipped his arm around her waist and pulled her to him. She pulled his hand off her, grimly thanking the server before hurrying to the front door. She stepped out into the warm night air, hurried down the steps, and then made a mistake. She hesitated. The shortcut to her car was along a treed path. Normally she wouldn't have thought twice about taking the path, but she didn't fancy getting caught by this guy on her own, away from public sight.

"Hey! Where are you going so fast? I thought we'd take a stroll, you know, get to know each other a little better." The smell of cloying aftershave enveloped her and made her gag.

"I'm not interested!"

His slippery smile didn't shift an inch. "Come on, I don't believe that for a minute."

She shook her head in disbelief. "What can I say to convince you?"

"Nothing."

She turned to go, but he grabbed her arm. Before she could speak, she heard a familiar, deep, sexy voice call out.

"I think you should leave the lady alone!"

Both she and her date turned to see Cam step onto the pavement. She blushed as she realized he must have seen the whole thing.

The guy bristled, but withdrew his hand as Cam approached. He was taller than her date, and his eyes looked dangerous. His mouth formed a tight line and the street light glanced off the handsome planes of his face. For the first time, she thought how much tougher Cam was than he appeared. Normally, he had no need to show his strength. But here, now, he was.

"Says who?" the guy asked finally, stepping back under Cam's forceful glare.

"Says the lady. You don't need anyone else to say it, do you?" The warning was there, low in his voice. Her date shook his head and, without a further look at Charlotte, walked off to his flashy car.

They waited in silence as the man roared off down the street and out of town. Charlotte shuddered. "Thank you, Cam, but I could have managed."

"Yeah, you could have, you might have, but I thought it wouldn't hurt to lend a helping hand."

She bit her lip and nodded, trying to avoid that gaze which, while less angry, still held an expression she found hard to face.

She swallowed her pride. "Thank you. I appreciate it."

"No problem. I just happened to be walking past."

"Just happened?"

He grinned and thrust his hands in his pockets. "No. Tell the truth, I heard you were meeting your date here, and I thought I'd pass by, make sure you were okay, and get a nightcap at the beach bar."

"I'm a grown woman. Of course I was okay." Even as she said the words, she realized that, if it hadn't been for Cam, she might not have been okay.

But he didn't pick her up on it, just nodded. He glanced around. "Would you like to join me for a nightcap?"

"No, thanks. I think I've had enough for one night."

"Okay, I'll walk you back to your car." She shot him a glance. "It's on the way to the bar," he said, before she could object.

"Okay, thanks."

They fell into step and Charlotte was glad of the sheltering darkness of the trees as it hid her embarrassment. It was bad enough that Cam knew she'd been on a blind date, but even worse that it had gone so badly and she had to be rescued from it.

"I've been at the pub with Gabe. Zane was there earlier, too. I don't think there's anyone in Akaroa Gabe doesn't know." Although Cam rarely saw the need to fill a silence, he must have sensed how uncomfortable she was feeling. He fell silent for a few steps, but when she didn't say anything, he continued. "I guess I've been living on the edge of communities, shifting around so long, that I forget what it's like living in a small town."

They took a few more steps and passed out from the shadows onto the street. To one side was her car, to her other side was the bar, bright lights piercing the darkness, with the sound of laughter and blues drifting across to them.

"It's nice," she said at last.

He turned to her. "What's nice?"

"Living in a small town. I spent my life in Wellington, which is a city with a small-town vibe. But I wanted to leave behind my father, try life on my own terms."

"And so you found your way here."

"Yes. Rachel encouraged me to come. She said it was a good place to make a new start."

"It is."

She nodded. "Yes, I like what I've found here." Her gaze suddenly hooked on Cam's and she felt a blush develop. Partly because neither of them appeared to be able to look away, and partly because she suddenly thought he might have thought she meant she liked *him*. She cleared her throat, her eyes unable to shift from his. "The small-town thing, I mean. I like it."

His face fell a little, barely perceptibly. She wouldn't have noticed if she hadn't have been so close. He stepped away abruptly. She felt her smile slip. He looked around with a rare look of confusion on his face, his eyes darting around as if looking for escape.

"What's wrong?"

His darting gaze once more rested on her. "Do you really want to know?"

"Yes, I wouldn't have asked if I didn't!"

He huffed a laugh. "I suppose so. You *are* a lawyer, aren't you?" He considered for a moment and then sighed. "Charlie, the reason I'm jumping around as if I've just been scalded is because I have an urge to push my fingers through that beautifully coiffed hair, loosen it and kiss those pouting lips."

She pressed the back of her fingers against her lips. Whether to protect them from a kiss or to imagine her fingers were his lips, she didn't know.

"Oh," she said.

He raised an eyebrow. "Is that it? Oh?"

She shook her head, desperately trying to rid herself of her errant thoughts which imagined him doing exactly as he'd described. "I don't pout."

He grinned. "You may not mean to, but…" His gaze fell to her lips. He licked his own lips before meetings her eyes again. "But they have a natural pout. Believe me. I've studied them."

"Oh," she said again, at a loss for words for once.

"I didn't want to come across like that other guy." He nodded toward where her date had last been seen.

That shook her out of her reverie. "You're nothing like that guy." The last of her doubts were swept away in the evening breeze. Now all she could see was Cam, in front of her, wanting the same thing as her, but not prepared to act on it in case he took a false step. So it was up to her to take that step. And she did. Toward him.

"He was a jerk. You're not," she said. Cam's sexy smile was

back in place. "In fact..." She reached up and pushed her fingers through his hair—something she'd been wanting to do from the very first moment she'd seen him. "I had the same thoughts as you, so maybe we *should* act on them."

She caressed his face with her thumbs as she searched his eyes for an answer. He lifted her chin with a slight touch of his finger.

"I think we should. In fact, it would be wrong not to."

He brushed his lips against hers with a soft sweep. His sharp intake of breath changed the passing touch to a gentle pressure of his lips against hers. It was as if his touch triggered every nerve ending in her body, and she could have sworn her skin shimmered in the shadowy light. She opened her mouth as her desire ratcheted up, wanting the feel of his tongue against hers. Instead, she felt his lips curve into a smile and he pulled away.

"Um," he said, his voice a sexy rumble which she felt deep inside of her. "That was even better than I imagined, and I'd imagined a lot."

He took her hand and kissed it. He continued to clasp her hand, as if he was scared she'd make a run for it.

"Would you like to change your mind about the nightcap?"

She nodded and, hand in hand, they walked toward the bar. It should have felt strange, it should have felt wrong, but, for the first time in a very long time, Charlotte felt completely right. The warm night, pleasure still flowing through her veins and the feel of Cam's hand clasping hers. She felt desired, she felt cosseted—she felt absolutely right.

"It's a long time since I've walked with someone like this," she said, feeling suddenly shy.

He glanced at her. A thrill of desire ran through her, banishing the shyness. He'd always had that effect on her, but now he was so much closer to her, the effect was amplified.

"That's a shame. But I'm sort of glad, too."

"Glad?"

"Yeah. The macho part of me is glad that I'm not just one in a long line of men."

"No, you're definitely not one of many."

He grinned, stopped walking, and gently tugged her to him. The sea lay dark, glittering under the warm breeze, which ruffled its surface.

He brushed her hair back from her face. "Not one of many? So that makes me special, eh? I like *that* even more."

She opened her mouth to deny it, but she didn't lie, so couldn't refute his claim. Not when all she wanted was for his lips to be pressed against hers. But he didn't kiss her, simply searched her face with a slight frown.

"What are you thinking?" she asked.

He glanced at her. "Trying to press the moment into my mind so I don't forget any of the details."

"Forget?"

"Yes, after I leave. I want to remember you, this moment, exactly as it is now."

It was like a savage kick in the guts. She had to stop herself from doubling up. She pulled away and looked out to the sea, temporarily darkened by a passing cloud.

"Of course," she said, a little curtly. "You're leaving after Christmas."

"Yes, you knew that," he said, sounding puzzled.

What the hell was she thinking? She shook her head. But she knew. She hadn't been thinking at all, and that had been her mistake. She inhaled a deep breath and turned to him. "Yes, but I'd forgotten." She glanced at where she'd parked her car. "I think I'll take a rain check on that night cap, thanks."

He grunted in sudden understanding. "Sure."

"Goodnight," she said, walking away.

"Goodnight, Charlie. And, if nothing else, do me a favor and quit the blind dates."

She paused in mid-stride but continued on with a brief wave of acknowledgement. He could take that how he wanted to. He was leaving, she was staying and therefore he had no business to influence her one way or another. And he especially had no business kissing her.

4

Cam steadied his balance on the stepladder as he reached up to the highest lantern, which had evaded attention for years. He sprayed some solvent on the rusting and broken metal, and gently loosened it, exposing the long-defunct bulb. He let out a quiet sigh as he looked at the bulb, knowing that the last person to have touched it was his mother. Ten years was a long time, but it felt like yesterday.

It had been a summer's day, just like this. He had stood at the base of the same ladder, steadying it for her as she'd replaced the bulb. She'd been wearing faded jeans and a white shirt with her hair piled up into a messy bun. She'd been a beautiful woman who'd remained youthful even into her later years. He couldn't remember what she'd called down to him. Whatever it was, he hadn't answered. So she'd teased him and turned to look at him, while the sun filtered through the trees above her, making her too bright to see her features clearly. He still had difficulty remembering her when he tried hard. But, occasionally, when he dreamed about her, he remembered her face clearly. He was glad he had his dreams.

With a firm grip around the bulb, he released it from its socket, tossed it to one side and replaced it with a new one. He twisted it into place and carefully replaced the shade.

"Okay, Dad," he called. "Turn it on."

"Right-oh!" replied Jim, who was standing at the ready, peering out of the kitchen window, his fingers hovering over the light switches.

Suddenly the darkened canopy of trees and garden was transformed from something moody and mysterious to something welcoming and happy, as all the lights turned on, filling the garden with magic. By the time Cam reached the bottom of the ladder, Jim was there, gazing around the garden with a big, soppy smile.

"I can't remember the last time they were all lit like this."

Cam picked up an old towel and wiped his hands free of some of the solution he'd used to loosen the metal clamps. He eyed his father with a wry smile.

"They're always on, Dad. I was surprised you could turn them off at all."

"They're always *turned* on, but there hasn't been a complete set for years. I kept meaning to do it, your brothers kept meaning to do it, but you actually did it."

Cam looked away, suddenly embarrassed, as if his feelings for his mother had been revealed by his actions. If there was one thing he didn't like to do, it was to show his feelings. He corrected himself. No, what he didn't like to do was actually *have* any feelings.

"I'm leaving soon. I wanted to get it done before I left."

Jim looked from the lights to Cam. Cam could still see the sentimentality in his eyes, and he inwardly groaned.

"Well," Cam continued, "I'd best get on."

Then he felt his father's large hand, gnarled a little now with arthritis. It pained him to see his father getting older. It had come as something of a shock after being away for so long. His father squeezed his hand around his arm.

"You don't have to go."

"I do. We should leave soon."

"You know what I mean. You don't have to leave Belendroit, me, the family, New Zealand."

Something gripped Cam's gut, a hardening around something he didn't want to feel. It needed to be contained. "I have a life overseas."

"Do you?"

Cam blinked and slowly turned to face his father. "You know I do."

"You might have things to do, but I worry about you, son. You, out of all my children, are the most like your mother. And you, out of all my children, have the closest affinity to Belendroit, exactly as your mother had."

It was true, and Cam knew it. He'd watched with surprise as his brothers and sisters came and went from Belendroit. It was a place dear to all of them, but he knew he felt it more deeply than them. Anyone else would have called it love. But Cam didn't. He didn't call anything love. He refused to go there.

Cam shrugged. "Zane's done a lot around the garden."

Jim snorted. "Most of it to impress Rachel. But it's true he worked hard."

"And David. He got the drive leveled."

Jim frowned this time. "I didn't even *want* it leveled. Typical David! He just assumed I did."

"It's saved our cars from getting stuck, and remember what happened with Amber's mini?"

"Yes, I know it was for the best," Jim grumbled. "Everyone leaps in and levels this, demolishes that, pulls out the other. But you, you do everything with great sensitivity. Like those bulbs. No one else thought to do it that way. They'd have ripped them all out and stuck up a replacement. But by mending the parts, you've preserved them for the future. Just as my lovely Catherine would have done."

A weakening wave of emotion washed through him. He cleared his throat, trying to clear away the unwanted feelings.

"It's true," he said, looking around at the garden, transformed by the lights and at the house, sitting snug and happily amongst the trees with the sea close behind it, murmuring in the evening's quiet. "But I have work to do overseas."

They fell into step as they walked back to the house.

"You have work to do here, too. Zane was telling me about how you're helping Charlotte out with the Waitahi project."

Cam drew in a sharp breath at the unexpected mention of Charlotte.

"Well, I'm here. I know a bit about it, so I thought it was the least I could do."

Jim laughed. "I guess it doesn't hurt that Charlotte is one of the most beautiful women I've seen." He frowned a little. "True, she's a little on the cold side."

Cam stopped dead in his tracks. "Cold?" he spluttered, surprised and irritated at the description of Charlotte. "She's not cold. How could you think she's cold?"

Jim shot Cam a knowing look, but continued walking up the steps and onto the veranda. It wasn't until he took his usual seat at the corner of the veranda, so he could see both the sea behind the house and the trees at the front, that he spoke again.

Jim leaned back in his chair and surveyed his son with a look which was uncharacteristically complex. Cam's resolve folded under his scrutiny and he followed him onto the veranda and leaned against the pillar.

"Maybe you're right, son." Jim shrugged. "But I've known the woman for a year or so now, since she arrived in Akaroa, and she's certainly not someone who invites closeness. Or she's not to me, anyway."

Cam cocked his head to one side. "What are you insinuating, Dad?"

"I'm not insinuating anything. I'm *suggesting* that maybe she's showing you a softer side, that's all." He nodded his head slowly. "And I have to say that that could be something worth seeing."

Cam pushed himself off the pillar and made a scoffing sound. "My father, the expert on women."

"What can I say? I like women, but no matter the odd flirtation, there was only ever one woman I loved, and that was your mother."

"I don't know how she put up with you."

"Because she understood me better than I understood myself. That's how. But, anyway, we're talking about the lovely Charlotte. So what's she like, really? Behind that glacial facade."

Cam shook his head at the description, which was so far off the mark that it wasn't funny.

"What's she like?" He looked up at the string of lights punctuating the darkened branches. "She's everything she appears—smart, with integrity, beautiful—and more." The lights swam out of focus and his eyes watered a little. He must be tired.

"More?" his father prompted.

Cam looked back at his father. "She's also the most intriguing woman I've ever met. She's so full of power and yet so full of sadness." His eyes narrowed as he remembered the glimpses of the vulnerability he'd seen inside. "That it hurts." He rubbed his stomach as if to stem the ache which he felt when he thought of her hidden vulnerability.

His father smiled and shook his head. "Your mother always said you had too much EQ for your own good." He paused. "Emotional Quotient, like IQ, except it's about your emotions."

"I know what EQ is, Dad."

"Then why do you pretend you don't have any? Why do you suppress your emotions so much that you no longer believe you have them? Because, son," Jim said, wearily rising to his feet and placing his hand on Cam's shoulder, "you *do* have them, and the best way to deal with them is embrace them, rather than suppress them. Because when you try to stop them, weird things happen—they twist and get out of shape."

Cam's mouth tightened. He didn't want this conversation. "Right, thanks, Dad, for your psychoanalysis. Text book description."

"You're welcome, son." Jim turned away and Cam closed his eyes, willing his father not to continue the conversation. But Jim only made it to the door before turning and talking to Cam's back. "But, believe me, Cam, if you get a chance to love and be loved, take it. Because it's rare and fleeting and is immeasurably valuable. In fact, it's the only thing in life worth valuing."

Cam kept his eyes closed as he listened to his father walk down the hall to his bedroom to get ready for the community meeting, which he'd agreed to drive his father to, since he'd decided night driving was too taxing for his eyes. He, too, should get ready.

But, instead of following him, Cam sat outside, in the chair he used, next to his father's. This chair didn't look out to the sea, but inland, to the trees and hills upon which the last strands of the sunset could be seen. He never tired of the view. But now all he could think of was how, with very hour he stayed at Belendroit, every moment he spent with Charlotte, the roots of family and home tightened around him, drawing him closer, exposing his heart a little more to danger.

And he knew how to counter danger. Remove himself from it. And that was exactly what he'd do. He'd still leave in the New Year and return to his old life, unencumbered by anything. But before he went, he wanted to make things a little better for Charlotte if he could. He wanted her to see what a remarkable woman she was—with or without her father's approval.

CHARLOTTE HAD ARRIVED EARLY in Flo's dining room—it seemed everyone, including Flo, had given up calling it a meeting room—and was waiting for the last few stragglers of the community council to arrive. She'd jumped at the opportunity to chair the committee when the role became vacant and hadn't regretted her decision. Since she'd joined the committee, she really felt like she was a part of the community, and was looking forward to nailing down the details of the Twilight Christmas Market, which was a highlight of Akaroa's Christmas festivities.

To her left sat Lynda, who owned the local craft shop, knitting baby clothes, and to her right was a young woman with a shaved head, pierced nose and tattoos peeping out from beneath her battered denim jacket. This was Etta, Rachel's daughter. Etta had had a complete image change a few months' ago when she'd come out as being gay, which had surprised no one in her extended family. Rachel seemed more perturbed by the shaved head than anything else.

"Is everyone here?" Charlotte asked, looking around.

"We're just waiting for Grandad," said Etta.

Lynda turned her knitting around. "He said he'd be a bit late. He had a hospital appointment."

It did not surprise Charlotte that everyone knew Jim's business. Jim was that kind of man, and Akaroa was that type of community.

"Okay, then let's make a start on the routine business." Charlotte glanced at her watch. "Otherwise we'll run late." She nodded to Etta, who was going to update them on the rainbow parade which was planned for next year. Etta jumped up and held up a series of posters and began describing the events they portrayed with an authority that commanded the room.

Charlotte stifled her annoyance that the room still had none of the AV equipment which she was accustomed to. But no one else seemed to mind. The only thing they *had* minded was the idea of moving the meeting from Flo's place. Especially Etta, who worked part-time for Flo and considered it to be her second home. Even more so now her uncle Rob Connelly had married Flo. It seemed the Connellys were slowly taking over everything, including Charlotte's head.

Charlotte sighed as her mind drifted from Etta's explanation of how the rainbow procession would be organized to one Connelly in particular, who hadn't left her mind for what felt like a minute since the night, two days ago, when they'd kissed. Somehow she'd let her guard down with him, only to be forced to surface when he'd inadvertently reminded her he would be leaving in a few weeks. How could she have fallen for him so easily? She was beyond annoyed with herself. She tapped her pen sharply on the table in annoyance.

"What's up, Charlotte?" asked Etta.

Charlotte was suddenly aware everyone was looking at her as she flicked her pen back and forth like a cat's angry tail on the desk. She set it down. "Sorry, please go on."

"That's my bit done. The next item on the agenda is the children's carol singing. So I'll leave that up to Uncle Cam."

Charlotte's head shot around to see Cam had entered the room with Jim and was looking at her with his usual intense gaze. She desperately tried to quell a blush, but failed.

"Cameron! So..." She quickly pulled herself together. "So do you have anything to report?"

"About what?" he said in his usual, low, unhurried, sexy voice. It was all Charlotte could do to not purr under its caress. Unfortunately, the caress made her mind go blank.

"The... the Christmas entertainment."

"Which one, Charlie? Are you going to dress as a Christmas elf? Because I, for one, would give good money to see that."

His smile broadened, and her blush deepened. She looked around to see everyone looking intently from Cam back to Charlotte. Even Lynda's knitting needles had stopped their clacking and raised in the air, a dropped stitch uncaught and unnoticed. Charlotte glared around the table and with an embarrassed cough or two, and the occasional suppressed laugh, everyone turned away from her.

"The children's carol singing, Cameron, as you well know. Etta says you want to do something different, but hasn't gone into detail."

She determinedly met his gaze, and he pushed himself away from the window and walked up the middle of the U-shaped table, stopping briefly in front of her. She lowered her gaze. Unfortunately, it meant it was in line with his hips. He wore a soft, old chambray shirt which was open over a t-shirt. His jeans were equally old, equally softened over time and—she inhaled quickly—were like a second skin. She swore under her breath and raised her eyes to his chest. Tanned skin lay exposed over his t-shirt, a few hairs curling up. She clenched her fists around her pen once more, as her imagination worked overtime, wondering what it would feel like to lay her hand flat across his chest, shifting her fingers over his skin, feeling its heat and the slow steady beat of his heart.

She raised her eyes further and met his smiling gaze. He knew what she was thinking. He leaned over. She held her breath, and he turned on the one piece of equipment there was, a bluetooth speaker which she'd brought with her at Etta's request. Then he stepped away, tapped his phone and the sound of the Twelve Days of Christmas filled the room. Except it wasn't anything like she knew it. Instead of a "partridge in a pear tree", there was a "pukeko in a ponga tree" and instead of "five gold rings' there were "five big fat pigs".

Cam laughed at her expression, which obviously conveyed her disbelief, and returned to his position by the window again. He seemed to prefer standing.

"We thought we'd put on something different this year, eh, Etta? A bit of Kiwiana mixed with the old favorites."

Charlotte cleared her throat. "I thought we'd agreed on the evening's entertainment." She looked around and settled on Lynda, whose distraction was betrayed by the way she'd knitted past the dropped stitch without noticing it. "Something traditional, we decided, if I remember correctly. Didn't we, Lynda?"

Lynda looked startled to have been brought into what was obviously shaping up to be a very different meeting. Lynda shrugged and looked to Cam, which annoyed Charlotte. She, Charlotte, was the chairperson. Cam was only here because his father didn't like driving at night. Come to think of it, why *was* Cam staying?

"It *is* traditional," said Cam. "And it's also distinctly Kiwi and a bit of fun."

"I think the original is best. So, as the committee had previously agreed on a traditional Christmas, perhaps you could re-consider. Lynda," Charlotte said, not wanting to give him the opportunity to argue back, "perhaps you could record that."

Lynda suddenly remembered her role as secretary to the committee, dropped her knitting in her lap and made a few scribbled notes. Charlotte sighed. She'd suggested it would be easier for Lynda to use some device—a laptop, a phone, anything which reflected the times they were living in—but Lynda had been firm. Pen and paper were the only thing she was comfortable with.

"Your Dad's going to be here, isn't he, Charlotte?" asked Etta.

Charlotte nodded. She guessed Etta had overheard Rachel talking to Zane. She hoped Etta hadn't heard anything else about the blind dates.

"Cool," said Etta. "Don't worry about a thing, Charlotte. He'll love the carols."

Charlotte frowned as Etta and Cam exchanged conspiratorial grins.

"It will be an entirely professional affair, Charlotte," Jim bellowed. "Don't you worry, I'll oversee it."

Jim's words only worried her more. But she'd figure something out. That was a problem for another day.

AFTER CAM DROPPED his father off at Belendroit, he went to the pub, where the committee had gone after the meeting. He was concerned about his father, who'd been having a few hospitals appointments lately, which he always glossed over with words like 'checks', 'routine', 'just making sure'. But Cam had seen Jim in quiet moments of reflection, which were quite unlike him. His mother had been given to reflection and introversion, his father wasn't. So why now?

Cam's thoughts slipped away as he entered the pub and

immediately saw Charlotte, head to head with Rachel. His heart sank. What was his beautiful sister concocting now for Charlotte? He nodded to Gabe and a few others as he made his way to the bar and ordered a beer.

The place was warm, the windows open and doors opened out onto a courtyard garden. Definitely different from the old days. Then it had been a workingman's place. Now it had been gentrified, and he wasn't sure how he felt about that. After a lifetime of being a maverick—an eccentric, on the outside looking in—finding himself mainstream was a shock.

His eyes settled on Charlotte. And how more mainstream could he get than falling for the town's solicitor? But he knew that was nothing was at it seemed. And that Charlotte was far more than she appeared to everyone else. Seeing her from the side, her face animated in conversation with Rachel as she leaned in, laughed and then sat back, sipping her wine as she listened to Rachel, he felt that damned stirring inside again. And it wasn't only the usual stirrings. Those he could easily deal with. The kind that Charlotte created inside of him was a different matter entirely.

Gabe beckoned him over, but he shook his head and gestured toward Rachel. Gabe shot him a big grin and returned to his table. He looked back at Rachel, who was poring over her phone, turning it to show Charlotte, and Cam felt a shot of anger. What the hell were they doing, looking for a perfect stranger to fill the role of Charlotte's fiancé? Cam might not be perfect, but he wasn't a stranger and he could no more bear the thought of Charlotte being courted by a different man than fly to the moon. No, it was time for some action.

. . .

ALTHOUGH CHARLOTTE HAD her back to the entrance, she knew the precise moment Cameron had entered the pub. It wasn't because people had looked up and greeted him, and it wasn't because Rachel had glanced from him to her with a raised eyebrow. It was because she could *feel* him—his eyes on her, his energy in the room. Whatever it was—and she certainly wasn't used to expressing herself in such metaphysical terms—she knew he was there and she knew he was aware of her in just the same way.

But she was determined to ignore him. She still felt unsettled at the personal way in which he'd addressed her at the meeting. She wasn't accustomed to feeling ruffled and exposing herself to the community to which she now belonged. And if he thought he could do that, mess with her feelings, and then leave, he had another think coming. So she continued to steadfastly refuse to follow her instincts and look his way and, instead, she focused on the prospective dates which Rachel was showing her.

"That one," she said decisively, as Rachel showed her a photo of an innocuous-looking man smiling at the camera with his head slightly dipped as if he'd just finished pushing his hair back through his fingers. "He'll do." She swiped right.

Rachel brought the screen back to her gaze and frowned. "Are you sure? He looks a little, well… timid, really."

"Timid is fine. In fact, timid is good. He won't mind being dominated by my father."

"And your dad will like that?" asked Rachel. Charlotte caught the incredulous tone in her voice.

"Are you kidding me? He'll love it. The only thing he likes better than an audience is to be superior to everyone in the room."

Rachel shrugged, switched off the phone, and slid it into her handbag. "Well, he's *your* date."

Charlotte raised her glass to Rachel's and clinked it. "He is. And here's to it being a good one."

"What are you two celebrating?"

Charlotte jumped as she looked up at Cam. His brow lowered a little as if something had annoyed him.

Rachel looked at Charlotte and raised an eyebrow. "Charlotte?"

Charlotte shook her head decisively. No way was she going to admit they'd just set up her second blind date.

Cam shrugged. "Oh well," he said, his frown disappearing as his gaze lingered on her—a gaze which triggered thousands of butterflies in her stomach. "Do you mind if I join you?" The politeness of his question was undermined by the fact he didn't wait for an answer before grabbing a chair from an adjoining table and sitting down. "Don't mind me. Carry on with your arrangements for Charlie's second date." He looked from Rachel to Charlotte. "Or is that settled now? Ah, yes, I guess that's what you were drinking to."

"Cam!" spluttered Rachel. "That's Charlotte's personal business, which she obviously doesn't want to discuss with you."

"Is that right?" he asked, looking at Charlotte.

"Yes, it is." She could feel her cheeks burning.

"Then we can change the subject. Let's talk about what? Rachel, any ideas?"

"Christmas!" said Rachel, obviously plucking the first thing she thought of out of the air. "Our favorite Christmas."

"Cool." Cam turned to Charlotte. "I'd love to hear your favorite Christmas story."

Charlotte swept her hand in a fashion which she hoped looked casual. Because there was nothing about any of her family Christmases she wished to share. "Oh, you know, the usual. Family presents."

"Is that it?" asked Cam.

She'd have to give him something. She thought for a few minutes. "Probably the most memorable was when we went to visit my grandparents in England. It was snowing outside and freezing inside this enormous house in the country. I remember the church bells ringing, and walking to this medieval stone church on a brilliant sunny day, but I couldn't figure out why the sun was so low and the light so different." She was lost for a moment, remembering the time. "My parents were together then, and both sets of grandparents were alive and there. It was… lovely."

She re-focused her gaze on Rachel and Cam, and saw they were both staring at her.

"How long after that did things change?" Rachel asked.

She blinked and pressed her lips together. "It never happened again. My mother and father separated shortly afterwards, my grandmother got dementia, my grandfather died. My other grandparents died in a car crash."

Rachel's mouth formed a worried O.

"And your Christmases after that?" Cam asked. "Who did you spend them with?"

"With my father and whoever was vying for the position of wife. At least for an hour or two until my father asked my nanny to take me away. It wasn't until I was older that I learned the things which triggered my father's anger."

"Like?"

"Anything to do with my achievements. It took me well into my twenties before I realized he only saw these as competition. But, by the time I'd discovered this, we'd drifted apart." She looked at them both, thinking they'd probably got more from her than they'd expected. "Anyway, I'd best be off. I think I've lowered the mood enough." Besides, she really didn't want to listen to them talking about all the Perfect Connelly Christmases they'd had together. She picked up her bag and stood up.

Cam also stood up. "I'll walk you home."

"There's no need."

"Does there have to be a need for everything?"

"Yes, there does." Ignoring Rachel's pleas for her to stay, she gave her friend a quick kiss on the cheek and walked away, hoping Cam wouldn't follow her. But she hadn't taken two steps out into the street before the door opened behind her, and she could hear the farewells shouted out to him through the open door before it clanged shut.

He ran to catch her up. She shivered in the night air, and he passed her cardigan to her.

"You were in such a hurry to leave you forgot this."

"Thank you." She should put it on, but instead she stood and looked at him. "Why do you constantly try to upset me? Do you get some kind of weird kick out of it?"

He grimaced, and she knew she was spot on. "I want a reaction from you, I guess. I want you to get angry with me, get angry with your father, do something to crack that facade you show to the world that hides the real you."

"But why would you want that? I don't understand. It's all I have between me and the world. It's my protection. Once that's gone, I have nothing."

He shook his head. "That's not true. You have everything. And you frustrate the hell out of me because you can't see it."

"So you think you need to tease me for my sake. To make me a better person."

He had the grace to look embarrassed. "Put it like that, and it sounds bad."

"That's because it *is* bad."

He pushed his fingers through his hair and shuffled his feet. "I'm doing this all wrong." He reached out and took her hands.

"What all wrong? What is it you really want, Cameron? I'd love to know."

"I'd love you to stop going out on blind dates."

She frowned. "Who are you to tell me to stop dating? You come here, into my life and think you can cause chaos and then leave again? It doesn't work like that."

"Then tell me how it does work," he breathed.

Tears pricked her eyes. "I don't know, Cam, I don't know."

"Then I will not give up, not until we both understand what the hell is happening."

He stepped away from her, then turned and walked away without a backward glance, leaving her feeling more confused than ever. And more determined to continue on her original path than ever. Confusion was the opposite of what she wanted in her life.

5

Every time the door to the wine bar opened, Charlotte looked up, wondering if it was her blind date. But only couples, or someone heading toward a group with a wave and cries of greeting, had entered so far. She felt as if she were the only person sitting alone in the whole place. Despite her reluctance to agree to Rachel's suggestion to give blind dating one more go, she'd agreed, and she knew why. Desperation. Time was running out, and she refused to admit to her father that she'd made up the whole fiancé thing. He'd think her even more fallible than he did already.

The door clanged again, and a nervous-looking man entered and looked around. He caught her eye and smiled in query. It must be him. She gave a quick nod. At least he didn't look as full of himself as the previous date. Quite the reverse.

"Hello," he said. He looked even less prepossessing upon a closer look. But looks weren't everything. Take Cam—he was gorgeous, but as prickly as a hedgehog. Stop thinking about Cam, she told herself firmly.

"Hello." She smiled.

"Would you like a drink?"

"I have one, thanks."

He nodded, hesitated awkwardly, and gestured to the bar. "I'll just go and, er, get one for myself then."

She looked down at her half-full glass of wine and hoped he'd bring back a bottle. But he hadn't asked her what she was drinking, so she somehow doubted it. She sighed. For once, it would be nice for someone to be aware of her needs and act on them without her having to ask. She watched the man waiting patiently behind a group of people who didn't seem about to move anytime soon. He pulled a face but didn't attempt to get closer to the crowded bar. She sighed and took another sip of her drink. She'd have to rescue him soon if no one else took pity on him. Just what she needed—a man who everyone pitied. And, if they pitied him, they'd certainly pity her. Especially her father. She finished her drink and stood up. She'd rescue her date, have a drink, and then leave.

She wove her way through the throng of people and suddenly found her way blocked. She looked up into blue eyes that were focused only on her.

"What are you doing here?" she said, throwing an alarmed look to where her date still stood, three back from the bar. He hadn't seen her, nor made any progress toward the bar.

Cam grinned. "Good to see you, too. I didn't expect to see you on your own, though. Rachel told me not to come, said you had a date."

"But you came anyway."

His grin didn't falter. "Course I did." He took her glass and held it up to the bar manager. "Phil! A bottle of Sauvignon Blanc, please!" His deep voice effortlessly carried across the heads of the people between them and the bar. It helped that he was taller than them, too.

"Sure, Cam!" called the man. "Take a seat and I'll bring it over."

"Cheers, mate."

Charlotte shot a frustrated gaze at her date, who still stood quietly, waiting for the crowds to part, oblivious to her presence.

"Is there anyone you Connellys don't know in Akaroa?"

He looked down with a slight smile. "Yes, you. But I'm going to remedy that. Come on, let's take a seat."

Charlotte couldn't fight her way over to where her date stood and so returned with Cam to the small table in the corner where she'd left her coat. There were only two seats.

"You can't sit there. My date is coming back from the bar any minute."

Cam looked around. "Which one is he?"

Charlotte didn't particularly want to point out her unimpressive date to Cam, so gestured vaguely. "Over by the bar."

"Tell you what, Charlie, I'll take a seat and when he comes back, I'll let him sit down. Okay?"

"I suppose so. But you're not staying."

"Here you go, Cam. Settle up later. Have a great night," the bar manager said with a wink after looking at Charlotte.

Charlotte crossed her arms and glared at Cam. "I don't know what you think you're doing, coming in here and trying to take over, knowing I have a date."

"As I said, Charlie," he said, sitting down and pouring them both a glass of wine, "I'm getting to know you. Trying to figure out why you're so desperate for a date on Christmas Eve."

"And why would you be bothered to do that?"

He shrugged, the smile unchanged. "Because I'm a nice man who wants to spread some happiness."

"More likely because you're nosy and want to know what's going on. Intrigued because I'm not interested."

"Oh, you *are* interested." He leaned across the table. "I can see it in your eyes whenever we're together. You react physically to me, and you react emotionally to me. And I definitely felt it when we kissed." He leaned even closer, and she had to lean in to catch what he was saying. "But, intellectually, you're holding back."

She was stunned for a moment before she rolled her eyes, all thought of her date by the bar forgotten. "How clever you are," she said facetiously. "Your life must be so easy when you're able to read people so accurately."

"No," he said, leaning back in his chair, his eyes narrowed as if assessing her. He took a sip of wine before answering further. "It doesn't make life easy being clever. You should know that."

"No, it doesn't. It makes life more difficult, if anything."

He reached out for her hand. "You're a wonderful woman, Charlie. You don't need to find a man to impress your father."

She tried to withdraw her hand, but only half-heartedly and it did feel nice, so she left it in his. She loved the feel of his hand over hers. It was the hand of someone who worked outside, calloused, but his fingers were long and tapered—musician's hands. And they were sensitive as they ran over her skin, sending skittering sensations throughout her body.

"Am I interrupting anything?"

She jumped and pulled her hand guiltily out of Cam's grip.

"No, sorry, I'd just met up with a friend. He was just going."

Cam rose and offered his chair to the man, but remained standing beside him, leaning against a pillar. It had the unfortunate effect of making Cam looking even more impressive beside the man, who sat looking from one to the other. After all that time, he'd bought only one glass of beer. He hadn't even gotten her a drink.

"I'm in no hurry," said Cam. He stuck out his hand to the

man. "Pleased to meet you... I'm sorry, I didn't catch your name."

The man stuck out his hand. "Alan. Alan Pritchard."

"Alan, I'm Cam. Sorry to have busted in on your date like this."

"No problem." But Charlotte could tell that was the last thing Alan thought.

"That's good," said Cam, pouring himself another glass of the wine he'd bought. "Charlie and I were just talking about her dates."

Alan looked from one to the other. "Oh?"

"Yes, I reckon she doesn't need to go on blind dates."

"I guess none of us really need to, but sometimes it's difficult to find someone in the course of your everyday life."

"Yes, I'm sure. What is it you do, Alan?"

"I'm a librarian. A children's librarian."

"Cool," said Cam.

"I love working with children. But, as you can guess, it's not so good for the dating. I don't get to meet many single women."

Cam laughed. "There must be some single moms amongst them."

Alan was beginning to sweat, and he brought out an old-fashioned handkerchief, monogrammed with his name in the corner, and wiped his forehead. The thought of flirting with the mothers appeared to have given Alan a bout of nerves.

"I haven't seen a hankie like that in years. Have you Charlie?"

She shook her head, wondering when on earth Cam was going to leave.

"It's from my mother. A box for Christmas." Alan gave a weak smile. "Every Christmas," he added ruefully.

"That's nice. My mother used to give me home-made things, too. But they were pretty quirky."

"What do you think she'll give you this Christmas?" Alan asked with interest.

"Cameron's mother passed away some years back," interjected Charlotte quickly.

"Oh, I'm sorry."

"Not half as much as me," said Cam wearily.

Charlotte had no choice but to reach out to Cam to show him some kind of comfort. "She was a wonderful woman, by all accounts," said Charlotte softly.

"She'd have loved you," said Cam, his eyes fixed on her once more.

She couldn't have torn her eyes from him if she'd wanted to. He held a depth of feeling in his eyes, complex with his aching heart for a mother who was taken away too soon, and something more. Something which was only for her. She couldn't have said how long their gazes were locked on each other. It was as if they were an island in the busyness of the wine bar. The sound and sights had receded, leaving only them and an unspoken connection.

A loud cough jerked her out of the connection. She turned to see Alan had stood up. He had a regretful smile on his face. "Looks as if I'm not needed here."

"Alan! I'm so sorry. I thought Cam was going."

"I think Cam should stay, don't you?"

"Good on you, mate," said Cam.

"No, Alan, please, stay."

"It's okay, Charlotte, really it is. I'm not sure what's going on between the two of you but I know it's not a blind date with me you need." He smiled and Charlotte felt terrible because he was a nice man, but she had eyes only for the annoying handsome one. And there didn't seem to be anything she could do about it. And she'd definitely not been able to hide it.

"I'm sorry, Alan. I hadn't meant for this to happen."

"No problems. It was lovely to have met you." He held out his hand, shook hers, and turned to do the same with Cam.

They both watched him walk away.

She groaned and pressed her hand to her forehead. "I feel terrible."

"Why? Alan seemed cool about it all."

"He was just being nice."

"You'd rather he wasn't nice?"

She jumped up. "Just stop it, Cam. Stop twisting my words, stop butting into my life." She grabbed her bag and jacket. "I'm leaving."

"Okay then," said Cam, grabbing the nearly full bottle of wine. "We can finish the wine at your place."

She shot him a dark look. "I'm going. And I'm going alone."

She pushed her way through the crowded room to the exit, only to find that Cam was right behind her.

"Cam! What are you doing?"

"I'll walk you home."

"I don't need anyone to walk me home, thank you. We went through this last night."

"Probably not. But my dad wouldn't be happy if I let you walk home alone. So, how about I just walk beside you, as I'm going that way anyway? We won't call it 'walking you home.'"

She shook her head and walked quickly away. Surely his laconic walk wouldn't be enough to catch her up. She was wrong. With his long legs, he only had to slightly pick up the pace to walk beside her. She was too annoyed with him at sabotaging her date to break the silence. And, it seemed, Cam was perfectly happy with the lack of conversation.

Her cottage was only a short walk away and when she stopped beside the white picket fence, Cam looked at the cottage, framed by trees, in surprise.

"I wondered where you lived."

She crossed her arms outside her gate. "Then how did you know you were going this way?"

"Because I was going whichever way you were." He leaned over the fence to get a better look. "Of all the places I imagined, this didn't come close."

"No, well, it was a bit of an impulse buy."

"An impulse straight from the heart." He looked at her and her heart stopped. "It suits you. What do you say I come inside, we finish the bottle and then I go home like a good chap, as my dad would say?"

She found herself nodding. She swallowed and looked around. "Sure." The longer they stood talking, the more likely her neighbors would spot them and the gossiping would begin.

She opened the small gate in the white picket fence. Yes, it was twee, yes she loved it, and yes, she was crazy for inviting him in. But it didn't seem as if she had any other choice. She was acting on impulse, and that impulse was too strong to deny.

She turned at the front door, and he nearly walked into her. She had to look up into his shadowy face. His lips parted slightly, and she gripped her keys and the door handle to stop herself from cupping his face and planting a big kiss on those perfectly formed lips.

"Just a few drinks and then you go. Right?"

"Right," he said, and she opened the door, knowing that the chances of that happening were extremely slim.

CAM FOLLOWED Charlotte into her house. He'd expected a pristine apartment. Something controlled and beautiful. He was half-right. It was a small, picture-perfect cottage, but inside it was all painted white with flashes of brightly colored cushions on the white sofa. Control and beauty within a cottage which must have had its origins in the nineteenth century. He had known that she was more than she appeared, but seeing her in her inner sanctum proved it.

Her house in Akaroa wasn't one of the prestigious ones perched on the side of the hill with views of the water—which he was in no doubt she could afford—nor was it a modern glass box. What it was, was a small cottage with roses around the door and a secluded private garden which bordered on the reserve. The thing that struck him most was the privacy of the place and how much it was like a picture book, children's version of a home.

"I'll get some glasses," she said.

He placed the bottle on the table and looked through the window into the garden through which they'd just walked, now lit by the porch light. He could see a summer house at the end of the garden between the trees.

"It's pretty," he said.

She laughed. "Don't sound so surprised. I have someone in to do the garden. I don't get my hands dirty."

He took her hand. "And such pretty hands, you're quite right. They made for doing other things." Her breath snagged, and she licked her lips. "Like what?"

He couldn't resist. He took her pretty hand and brought it to his lips and kissed each fingertip. He studied her fingers. Her nails were manicured and covered with a pale translucent gloss.

"Like being kissed."

"Cam," she said in a voice which was too soft and caressing to be a warning. "You said one drink and you'd leave."

"And I will." He allowed her fingers to slip from hers, sighed, and stepped away. "But you must admit, we do have something to celebrate."

He could see her relax a bit. "Yes, we do. And that's thanks to you. You've made this project into something I didn't think was possible."

"It's going to work, and it's going to work well. Especially with you to oversee the partnership."

"They want you to work on it, you know."

"I know. But it's not something I can do from a distance."

Her smile flickered, and she turned away, but impulsively he reached out and stopped her from walking off.

"It's just what I do, Charlotte." He used her full name for the first time. They both noticed.

"Maybe it's time to change. Maybe it's time to stop and see what that's like."

Denial was on his lips but he couldn't say the word, couldn't contradict her when all he wanted to do was kiss those lips and stay here, with her, right now. Maybe she could read his mind because she took a step closer to him. And for a moment they teetered on the edge of action, and the air thickened with intent.

Suddenly, the piercing sound of an incoming call filled the air.

For a moment, he didn't think she'd answer it. She was lost in a different place. But the insistent sound broke the spell, and she rummaged in her bag for her phone and answered it.

"Charlotte speaking," she said, in her usual efficient manner, without looking at the screen. But the instant she heard the voice on the other end of the phone, her manner changed. She stood taller and her fingers tightened around the phone, clasping it as if it might disappear.

"William!" she said, her voice tight with tension but happy, he could tell. She listened for a bit. "Everything okay?" she asked, her voice a little tentative now. Cam wondered at what point he had started to recognize the change in her tones, become sensitive to her reactions.

"Oh," she said, and he knew something had happened, something which had upset her. "But—" Whatever she'd been about to say had been interrupted. Cam could hear the deep, peremptory male tones dominate her. Instinctively, he took a step toward her—positioning himself so she could see him—and raised a questioning brow. She shook her head and twisted away from him, her eyes lowered and darting, as she listened to the other end of the phone while taking short breaths, as if she was about to speak but was constantly being interrupted. Finally, there was silence on the other end of the phone.

"Please, Father." It was all she said but to see the self-contained, confident woman he knew destroyed by some words from her father broke Cam's heart. He suddenly had an idea.

"Charlotte!" he exclaimed. "Who is it?"

Charlotte turned to him. "My father. He can't come after all."

Suddenly, he could hear her father talking once more.

"Okay," she said to her father, and she wiped her eyes quickly as she tapped the screen to allow a video call. It was just as Cam had expected. Her father's curiosity had got the better of him.

Cam put his arm around Charlotte's shoulders. "Aren't you going to introduce me?"

Charlotte shot him a confused look but turned to her father, who had suddenly turned on the charm.

"Father, this is Cameron Connelly."

Cam waited for a further explanation, but she didn't expand on their relationship.

He squeezed her shoulder and looked at her father with a smile. "Charlotte's fiancé. Good to meet you at last, sir. I was looking forward to meeting you in person at Christmas."

"Ah," Charlotte's father replied, the smile still broad over his aristocratic features, "that's why I rang. Charlotte's last message seemed to suggest you might not be able to make it after all. And, as I have something pressing..." He faded away as if it were something far too confidential and important to share.

"Darling," said Cam, kissing her cheek and enjoying the flush which bloomed under his lips. "I'm sorry. I forgot to tell you I can definitely be with you and your father on Christmas Eve. No problem. I was really hoping to see you and I know Charlotte was too, weren't you, darling?"

Charlotte drew away from the camera so that only Cam could see her eyes narrow in warning, but he ignored it. She turned to her father.

"Yes, I was, but if you can't come, then..." She trailed off. Cam had obviously given her a boost of confidence. It worked.

Her father leaned toward the camera decisively. "I'll have my secretary re-book the flights. I'll leave Clarissa here. She won't want to come." Cam doubted her father would have noticed Charlotte recoil at the insult, but he did.

"Of course," said Charlotte, tight-lipped. "I wouldn't want to put Clarissa out."

"She either wants to be in Auckland, Wellington, Sydney or London. You know how much she hates staying outside one of our homes."

Cam raised his eyebrows in surprise.

"Yes, I know. That's fine. I, I mean *we*"—she gave Cam a quick smile,—"look forward to seeing you Christmas Eve."

They said their farewells, and the screen went blank. Cam still had his hand on her shoulder. He thought he may as well continue playing the part while he could.

"Well, darling," he said, "looks like we have ourselves a date on Christmas Eve."

She huffed out an indignant sigh, turned away from the blank screen, lifted his hand and threw it off her.

"What the hell was that all about, Cam? What happened to the 'we have to be honest in our dealings with people,'" she said, in a voice mimicking his own, and not in a good way. "Hey?"

He shrugged. "Just trying to help."

"I don't *need* help."

"Looked to me like you did. You were practically begging him to come."

"And he wasn't going to, was he? Not until you said you'd be there as my fiancé."

He was getting confused. "That's what you wanted, wasn't it?"

"No, it wasn't!" Tears glittered in her eyes. She huffed again, exasperated, and pushed her hands through her hair, pulling it out of its neat twist. "What I wanted, Cam, was for my father to come and see *me*." She pressed her palm against her chest, right above her heart. "*Me*. His daughter. But he wasn't going to, was he? Do you know why?"

He could guess, but thought it better not to. He shook his head.

"Because he doesn't love me, because I've never been good enough for him. I never have, and I never will be."

He stepped forward, unable to stop himself, and gripped her arms.

"Charlotte, don't you see? You're too good for him. He may be your father, but he's no paragon of virtue. What I've seen just now is a man who is more interested in himself than you. But that's not down to you. It's him. Honestly? He's not worthy of your attention."

A tear trickled down her cheek. "And I suppose you think you are."

"I don't think. I *know* I am. Want to know why?"

She nodded, apparently unable to speak.

"Because I can see in every glance, in your every mannerism, what you're thinking and feeling. I can see it because we're in tune with each other and I feel you." He paused as her face crumpled and the tears flowed freely. "I don't think your father has a feeling bone in his body."

As soon as he'd uttered the last sentence, he knew he'd gone too far. She pulled away from him and stood at the table, clutching it, her shoulders heaving.

"I think you should leave," she said, in a broken voice.

"I don't want to leave you like this. Let me stay. We'll talk. We'll drink wine. We'll do whatever you like. Just let me stay here with you. I can't leave you like this," he repeated.

"Yes, you can. It's easy. You just go to the door, open it, step out and then close it again. Return to your busy family life and forget about me. You'll be doing that soon enough anyway, so I reckon you should do it right now."

"Make a stand with him. Your father, I mean. You can't let him run all over you."

"You don't know what you're talking about. *You* don't make a stand. Like my father, *you* just come and go. Selfishly following your whims."

He blenched at her accusations. "I make a stand every minute of every day. It's my mother's legacy and my curse."

"But you don't commit to it. You make your stand, then move on. I don't even know why you're here."

"Because I want to help you."

"How can you possibly think it'll help me for you to make love to me and then simply walk away? How can that help, Cam?"

It hit him then. She was right. He'd been fooling himself. He'd persuaded himself that all he wanted was to get her to recognize what a wonderful woman she was. But she was right. What he'd really wanted was to get closer to her because he was drawn to her like a magnet. He wanted her body, and he wanted her mind. He wanted her. Period. And how was that going to help her when he was leaving in a few short weeks?

"I'm sorry, Charlotte." He walked to the door and paused. "I'm really sorry. I didn't mean to make things worse."

He closed the door quietly behind him and walked up the path to the street and away from her. It was how it had to be. He'd thought he could help Charlotte, but all he'd done was make things worse for her—and a lot worse for him.

6

Cam never had problems concentrating. Never. Until now, that was. But, as he walked around the marshy land around the lake's edge with his newly recruited team of environmentalists who'd carry on the work after he'd left New Zealand, all he could think about was whether he was as selfish as Charlotte had accused him of being. Was he? Surely everything he'd done in his life so far proved otherwise?

He hated she believed he'd been toying with her from selfish motives only. But he hated even more that she might be right.

By the end of the morning, after nailing down the broader points of the plan to move forward with the work, he left the newly formed team excitedly talking about the future of the land. He had an appointment with a woman who he'd been determined to shake out of her shell. Trouble was, it appeared it had worked the other way around.

He twisted at the sound of a car horn beeping. Birds squawked and flew up from the scrubby trees. Flo's old car bounced over the rough ground towards him. His father waved from the front seat, as if Cam would have any problem spotting his larger-than-life father. As Flo had business in Christchurch she'd offered to take Jim to his hospital appointment.

Cam picked up his things and walked over to the car, checking his father's face for any sign of pain or discomfort. These mysterious hospital visits were beginning to alarm him. To begin with, Jim had described them as routine. But when pressed he'd become vague, which worried him. Not even Gabe, Amber or any of Cam's other sisters appeared to know more than him. Jim smiled back cheerily and Cam's anxiety waned as he jumped into the back seat.

"All right, Dad?" He squeezed his father's shoulder. His father shot him an affectionate look and placed his hand over Cam's.

"Of course. Right as rain."

Cam grunted, not deceived by the glib response. He'd have to keep his eyes open.

"Thanks, Flo. I appreciate the lift."

"No problem," she said, bouncing back toward the road. "Although I don't see why saving the planet means you can accept lifts but don't drive yourself," she grumbled, accelerating fast as she turned onto the straight road which led to the hills which divided Akaroa from Christchurch and the rest of the surrounding flat plains of Canterbury.

Cam opened his mouth to protest that he did drive but that he didn't see any point in adding to the number of cars on the road when Flo had arranged her day around taking Jim into Christchurch Hospital and bringing him back again. But before he could utter a word of protest, his father beat him to it.

"Straight to the heart of things as usual, Flo," said Jim, his loud voice easily heard over the straining engine of Flo's old car. She'd refused Rob's offer of buying her a new one. Rob claimed he couldn't understand his wife, but Cam suspected he did and that he was proud of her independence. Flo didn't have a materialistic bone in her body, and if the car could get her from A to B, then that was good enough for her. Even if, thought Cam as a puff of dark smoke billowed out of the exhaust as she overtook another "dawdling" car, it was hardly eco-friendly.

"Damn glad you're my daughter-in-law," continued Jim. "You'll keep all my errant sons straight."

"The others don't need keeping straight," muttered Flo, patting the glove box for her sunglasses as the sun pierced the clouds. "They have wives. It's only Cam who needs sorting out."

Cam groaned. "I *don't* need sorting. I'm sorted, thank you very much. And I've done it all by myself, would you believe?" he added facetiously. He'd known Flo since he was a boy and she'd been like a sister to him all his life. Now she was a sister-in-law, he didn't see any reason to treat her more politely. And, it seemed, neither did she.

She shot him a humor-filled look in the rear-view mirror. "Yes, I'd believe it."

He raised his eyebrow in quizzical disbelief. "You're agreeing with me?"

"Sure am," she said, crunching the gears as she shifted them down. The car dissolved into a roar as it overtook a truck which had pulled into the slow lane. Flo pressed the horn and waved in response. Cam didn't think he'd ever heard a car horn sound so friendly. He liked the fact that she could agree with him.

"Good."

But, there it came again, that look in the rear-view mirror, and he sighed, waiting for it.

"Of course you believe you've sorted yourself. Why wouldn't you?"

He waited for her to continue as she passed something to Jim, and they muttered between them. All too soon, she raised her voice to Cam over the straining engine.

"But you haven't. You only think you have. Because you're not seeing things clearly."

"Oh, come on, Flo. Give me a break."

"Ha! I will not! I'm your sister-in-law now. It's my role to *not* give you a break!"

Jim guffawed and Flo laughed, her infectious belly laugh, and Cam had no choice but to join in.

Eventually the laughter died down and Cam hoped the subject would change. He'd hoped in vain.

"What you need is a woman in your life." It seemed Flo would not give up. Perhaps if he remained silent, she'd stop.

"But who, Flo?" asked Jim, with a backward glance at Cam, which told him that Jim was playing along, feeding her lines. Cam pursed his lips and stared out the window.

"Miss Perfect, of course."

"Will you stop calling her that, Flo," said Cam, unable to prevent himself from responding in an irritated voice. He knew his answer gave him away.

"Why?"

"Because she's not... Well, she is, and she's not."

To Cam's concern, both Jim and Flo turned to look at him. When Flo turned back to look at the road, he relaxed a little. Jim continued to look at him, his bushy white brows beetled into confusion.

"What are you talking about, son? It's not like you to be flustered."

Cam gritted his teeth. There was only one subject which flustered him and that was Charlotte. "All I'm saying is that calling Charlie... Charlotte," he corrected himself. He'd be on a hiding to nothing if he let slip his pet name for her to Flo and his father. "That Charlotte isn't as she seems." He suspected that as little as he'd already said, it had been enough to give himself away.

To his surprise, neither Flo nor his father responded. Flo slowed as they drove through Akaroa, tooting the horn as she passed Amber's café. The silence felt heavy as he thought about Charlotte. How he was aware of everything nuance of her features, of every injustice done to her, of what a special woman she was, and of how filled with pain she was. Her need for her father's love and approbation showed how very different she was inside. And, most of all, he thought about how she'd accused him of being selfish. Just like her father. Her damned father. What he wouldn't give to have five minutes to tell him a few home truths!

"He must have given her a hell of a childhood," Cam muttered.

"Who gave who a hell of a childhood?" Jim asked. It was only then that Cam realized he'd spoken his thoughts out loud. But it was too late to backtrack, and besides, he wanted them to know.

"From the little Charlotte has said, and the gaping hole that's been in left in her psyche, I know her father must have completely ignored or undermined her, or been so self-absorbed that he never showed her any love." He grunted and looked out to the wooded promontory of Belendroit. "And that's why she appears so perfect on the outside, because she's trying to cover up the fact that she's hurting on the inside."

"Oh," said Flo on a short exhale of breath, as if she'd been winded. He met her understanding gaze in the rear vision mirror and waited for her to speak. Flo never only gave a one-word reply. But, it appeared, this time she did.

"That's terrible," said Jim. "Selfish people like her father should never be allowed to have children. Poor girl. What can we do to help her?"

"I'm working on it. I want her to see that she doesn't need her father's approval, doesn't need anyone's, that she's more than enough as she is."

"And how's that going?" asked Jim.

"Badly," he admitted.

"It's her life, Cam," said Flo in a gentle voice. "And you're leaving, so why not leave her be?"

"*Because*," he said, with more emphasis "she's not being true to herself."

"Why should you care?"

"Is there ever any good reason why people care? They either do, or they don't."

"And you do," said Flo quietly.

He shrugged. "I care about a lot of things. The land—"

"Especially around here," said Jim interrupted quietly. "Especially Belendroit."

"And I care for you lot, too. Though God knows why."

"As you say, Cam," said Flo. "You can't pick who or what you care for. You just do." She parked up the car and twisted in her seat to face him. "In which case wouldn't it be sensible to be with the things and people you care about?"

He'd intended to glare at her, but he couldn't hold her honest gaze, and looked away. "I can't stay at home."

"Why not?"

"Because I have things to do in England."

"Listen to yourself, Cam!" said Jim, exasperated. "You talk of Belendroit as home, and England as well, England. Your home is here, with us. With the people and places you love."

Cam grunted dismissively. He wished they'd both leave him alone.

"Ha!" said Flo. "You're as delusional as Miss Perfect."

Jim shot Flo a warning look, before looking back at Cam with a softer expression. He obviously thought Flo's bluntness had gone a bit too far this time.

"Isn't it time you stopped running away, son?"

It was as if the person he'd so carefully crafted all these years was beginning to fracture and Cam felt waves of emotion welling up, threatening to unbalance him. He hated feeling unbalanced. He hated feeling out of control.

He flung open the car door, jumped out into the drive and walked around to help his father out. He gulped in a lungful of fresh air, gripped the door, and poked his head inside to meet Flo's challenging gaze. "Thanks for the lift, Flo. I appreciate it."

"No problem. I'll see you later at the Twilight Christmas Market. Everyone will be there. Including Miss Perfect. Take my advice and follow your heart, not your head."

He ground his teeth in annoyance. Was the whole damned world conspiring against him?

"You can't keep on running, son," his father chipped in. "You can't keep on leaving and avoiding the one thing you need to address."

Cam shook his head and walked away without saying anything further. He swore under his breath at his father, at Flo, even at Charlotte, at the entire world intent on getting him to face the one thing he didn't want to face—making himself vulnerable to love. Because he was scared to death it would break him.

THE SUN HAD SET, leaving behind a violet haze which deepened with each passing minute over the peaceful harbor. But along the streets of Akaroa and in the park, the place was buzzing. Everything that could be lit up was lit up and music filled the air. People had come from all over Canterbury to celebrate the beginning of the summer holidays and to buy last-minute gifts from the market, which was packed full of artisan products, local foods and crafts. It was as if the entire population of the South Island had piled into Akaroa for the evening.

Or nearly the entire population, thought Charlotte, as she tried to focus on clearing away the last of her paperwork from her centrally located office. It was difficult when the local Scottish bagpipe band had set themselves up on the pavement across the way. She continued to work because she knew there would be a lot more after the weekend.

Eventually she called it a day and went outside into the warm evening. But the holiday atmosphere didn't rub off onto her like she'd hoped it might. Cam filled both her head and her heart.

She queued up at Flo's stall and ordered a coffee from Flo's assistant, while Flo chatted to the person in the line ahead of her. Her mind inevitably wandered back to Cam again.

She shouldn't have told him he was selfish. Yes, he was running from his own demons and had created his world to protect himself. Was that selfish or simply self-preservation? But the bottom line was that he was nothing like her father. And for that, she needed to apologize.

"Charlotte! Do you want some cake to go with the coffee or not?" asked Flo.

"Yes, sorry, I was miles away."

"I bet you were," said Flo, with a knowing look.

Charlotte sighed. She knew what Flo meant. Flo was never one to mince her words and had had a 'frank' discussion with Charlotte earlier about Cam. The discussion had only made Charlotte feel worse. She'd hurt Cam, and she'd only done it because she, herself, was hurting under his honest appraisal.

While she waited for Flo to put a slice of Christmas cake onto a paper plate, she looked around for him. He wasn't anywhere to be seen. When she turned back, Flo was holding the plate out to her with a quizzical look on her face. "If you're looking for Cam, you're looking in the wrong direction." She nodded her head to the edge of the market. "He's just arrived. Late as usual."

Charlotte glanced at Cam and then took her cake and coffee back to the table where Rachel and the rest of her family were seated. She focused on the conversation, ignoring the fact that she could sense Cam coming over her way. He greeted his family but refused the offered seat.

"You're making the place untidy, Cam! Come and join us," said Rachel.

"No thanks. I'll look around."

But he didn't move. Instead, he allowed his gaze to rest on Charlotte. She took pity on him, and rose and walked over to him. She owed him an apology. Why not get it over with? His face relaxed into a smile.

"Have you got a minute, Charlie? Fancy a walk around the stalls?"

"Sure."

"I'm sorry," they both said to each other at the same time.

"You first," said Charlotte.

Cam nodded as they walked past all the stalls they were meant to be looking at. "I'm sorry I said the things I said. But I'm frustrated that you don't see yourself as I see you."

They'd reached the edge of the open-air market and found themselves by the sea wall. Here, further away from the music, the sound of the sea gently lapping the shore and the call of birds beginning their nightly hunt filled the air. It was lulling and seductive enough to overcome her reservations. She couldn't resist.

"And how do you see me?"

He reached across, pushing her hair from her face, but kept the palm of his hand on her cheek. His thumb brushed her cheek gently and yet she felt his touch so intensely that it caused shivers of delight to run through her body.

"Pretty darn wonderful," he said, with a smile.

She smiled back, but then caught herself and took his hand reluctantly from her cheek. But he still held her hand, twisting his fingers around hers.

"But you're still leaving," she said in a whisper.

He nodded. "Yes, because that's what selfish people do."

She shook her head. "You're not selfish. That was anger speaking."

"Whatever was speaking, it spoke the truth. I am."

"No, you're not. You're right. You do so much for people and the environment. That's not the work of someone who's selfish."

"It is if it's what I want, too. No, Charlie, you were right. I *am* selfish and I can't see any other way around it because without that selfishness..." He shook his head.

"What?"

"I lose my guard against the world. My selfishness is my last defense."

"Defense? Against what?"

"Feeling something. *Anything*." He was silent as he groped for words, found some only to dismiss them again. If there were any words he didn't know them, because how could he talk about things he made sure he didn't even think about?

She ground her teeth to curb her sense of frustration. It didn't work. "And do you really think it's good to continue to repress your feelings?"

"No, but I'm going to do it, anyway. It's the only thing I know."

Her heart sank, and she pulled her hand from his. "Right." She looked away, anywhere but at him. "I think we should get back to the market."

He followed her gaze to the busyness of the town. "Why? Do you need some last-minute presents for your father?"

Hurt, she connected with his gaze once more.

"I'm sorry," he said quickly. "I didn't mean anything by that."

"Yes, you did. You never say anything you don't mean."

He pressed his lips together, and a muscle twitched in his jaw. "You're right," he said eventually. "I'm still frustrated that you need his approval. What can I do to make you see you don't need it?"

"You? Nothing. You're leaving in a few weeks. There's nothing you can do to change how I feel or what I want." The words came out more harshly than she'd intended, but it still annoyed her that Cam should insist she change to suit some concept he had of her, when he refused to make any changes himself.

"But this dating business. You won't go on any more, will you?"

She shrugged. "Rachel seems keen for me to have a third. She doesn't seem deterred even though I told her there was no point as he's already seen you. She said there's always a point in dating."

"Right."

He released her hand and huffed out a frustrated sigh. "I guess we're at an impasse. I'm not going to change and nor are you."

"You're leaving. Why should I change for you?"

"You don't get it. I don't want you to change for me. I want you to change for *you*. Isn't that enough?"

"Hey, Cam!" But Cam didn't take his eyes off her. Charlotte looked around to see Gabe waving at him.

"Looks like Gabe is trying to attract your attention." But he still didn't move. "Aren't you going to go over?"

"Not until you answer my question. Isn't it enough that you should change for yourself?"

"It's not that easy, Cam."

"Nothing worthwhile is."

"Hey, Cam!" said Gabe, running up to them. "Hi, Charlotte!"

'Hey, Gabe," she greeted.

"Cam, how's Dad? Did he say anything about his hospital visit?"

"I'd best be going," she said, making the most of Gabe's interruption to escape.

"Don't go," said Cam. "Not yet."

"Sorry," she said, backing away. "Got things to do. See you around."

Cam drew a deep breath and tugged his gaze from Charlotte's retreating. "No, he didn't say anything. I thought you might know more."

"I could if I pulled a few strings, but I was hoping he'd open up to you."

"No, he hasn't." His eyes drifted back to Charlotte, who'd been stopped by a group of people for a chat.

"I wasn't interrupting anything, was I?" Gabe asked. "Between you and Charlotte?"

Charlotte was standing beneath a flashing 'Merry Christmas' sign. Somehow, he didn't think either of them were going to have a particularly merry Christmas.

"No," he said, looking back at Gabe. "You weren't interrupting anything. I could have talked until I was blue in the face and I wouldn't be able to get through to her."

"Perhaps that's where you're going wrong, bro. Sweet talking a lady doesn't usually mean trying to browbeat her into submission. I reckon you could learn a few tricks from our niece," said Gabe. He nodded over to a stall which he hadn't noticed before. Rows of handmade ear-rings were strung alongside feathery dreamcatchers and wind chimes which tinkled in the warm breeze. Behind them, Etta had her arm hooked casually around a girl with long blonde hair and was chatting away while the girl looked up at her with a big grin.

"That's the girl she was telling me about," said Cam, impressed. "You're right. She works fast."

Gabe slapped him on the back. "Watch and learn, mate. Anyway, I'd best get back to give Maddy a break. Catch you later."

Cam looked around. He thought about joining Rachel and her family, considered going to say 'hi' to Amber who had a stall showcasing her paintings, even thought about having a drink with Ian, Flo's father, who was selling some of his home-made wines. But, in the end, he did none of these things. Because he looked across at Charlotte, who hadn't been allowed to progress any further than Lynda at the wool stall, and his heart stopped. She was listening to Lynda as she ran her hand over the stall's contents, plucking a baby's pair of booties into the air before smoothing her fingers lovingly along the fine wool and the ribbons. Something proprietorial overcame him and he knew then and there that he couldn't give up on her. He didn't know what the future had in store for him, but he knew what tomorrow did.

He turned and went in search of Rachel.

he following day, Charlotte found herself at Rachel and Zane's marae. She'd been summoned. She'd have preferred to remain at home, even if she had to be by herself. But she'd decided that things were getting bad if she preferred to be alone, rather than with friends. And it was this which had made her accept Rachel's request for a visit without bothering to look for excuses.

Children ran around the marae and Charlotte wondered if she'd ever have any. She watched as Rachel made her way back to the veranda after dropping off some baking to Zane's mother, who was ninety if she was a day and was recovering from a cold.

Despite Rachel's glamorous persona, her friend had made a wonderful home with Zane and Etta—her child she'd re-found after she had been adopted out so many years earlier— and now with her own baby. The old homestead in which Zane had lived as a bachelor had been completely trans-formed into the grand old homestead it had once been. Charlotte and Rachel shared similar tastes, and she appreciated the subtle design touches Rachel had added to the place. It was both a home, and a house which magazine editors were dying to do a feature on. But Zane refused point blank. Unlike his glamorous wife, Zane hated living his life in the public eye.

"You look pensive," said Rachel, standing alongside Charlotte.

"Do I? No, not really. I was just admiring your home and thinking what a lovely life you have out here. It's a lot different to your life in Wellington, when we'd hang out at cocktail parties and formal black-tie dinners."

Rachel pulled a face. "I don't miss that social scene at all." She cocked her head to one side. "You don't regret taking my advice and moving to Akaroa?"

"No, not at all. It's just..." She grimaced.

"What?"

"Just that I'm still trying to get my life together."

"It's early days." Rachel sipped her coffee and looked out to the hills which separated the valley from Belendroit and the sea. "Now I've done my familial duties with Zane's mum, you can tell me how your second blind date went."

Charlotte groaned. "It was terrible. Not least because your brother showed up and took over."

Rachel tutted but didn't seem too distressed at her brother's actions. "And so, how did that end up?"

Charlotte shrugged. She loved Rachel but wasn't about to confide everything that happened. Some things had to remain private. Besides, she wasn't so sure that Rachel wouldn't intervene if she saw fit and have a word with Cam. No, she had to keep her feelings to herself. "We had a few drinks, and he went home. That's all."

"Hm," Rachel said, as if Charlotte had just informed her of something very unsatisfactory. "Just a few drinks. Didn't he walk you home? Dad always instilled in his sons that they should be chivalrous and walk a girl home at the end of the evening."

"I thought he'd made that up!" exclaimed Charlotte, before she could sensor herself.

"Ah, so there was a bit more to it than you're letting on."

Charlotte shrugged. "Maybe."

"I see." And Charlotte could tell from Rachel's tone that she'd read between the lines. "So, that's good then." Before Charlotte could ask Rachel why that was so good, Rachel continued. "So I've set you up with a third date."

"No! Enough of these dates."

"This is someone I know will be a good fit. Honestly, Charlotte, I'm not palming you off with someone who sounds good on the phone but turns out to be a loser in real life. This time, I think it might work."

"There's no point now. I don't think my father is going to show up, anyway." And, she thought to herself, if he did show up, he'd be expecting Cam. "Let's leave it."

Rachel swept her hand in the air. "Forget about the fictitious fiancé by all means, but don't cancel this date. I think this one has potential."

"Okay." Charlotte didn't feel she had the strength to resist Rachel when she was on a mission. "So, what's his name? What does he do? Give me some details."

"No way. It's still a blind date. You turn up at the quay Saturday afternoon at four, go to the end, and you'll find him there."

"That's tomorrow."

"It is."

"The quay? Why there? Ah, the café, I guess."

Rachel shrugged and looked out into the distance, sheltering her eyes to better see her eldest daughter Etta rev her motorbike over the path and down into the valley. Rachel sighed. "She's such a tomboy. You know, I always imagined dressing up my daughter, doing her hair, getting her ready for parties."

Charlotte laughed, knowing both Rachel and Etta. They were like chalk and cheese, but they admired, respected, and loved each other for their differences. "And you got Etta instead."

"Yep." They watched as she jumped off her motorbike and took off her helmet, sweeping her fingers over her shaved head. Her nose ring glinted in the sunlight. Rachel's face broke into a wide smile. "I got my lovely Etta instead. And what a blessing she is. She's a remarkable woman."

Charlotte's heart faltered as she watched Etta look up at the house and wave at Rachel. Their bond was unmistakable, and she knew, hard won. She reached out and touched Rachel's shoulder.

"I have to go."

Rachel kissed her cheek. "Thanks for coming. It was great to see you here. Sometimes I think you avoid coming here."

"Why would I do that? You're my best friend."

Charlotte smiled, but Rachel didn't.

"Because you're looking for something, something you think I've found. And I have, Charlotte, and I don't blame you for avoiding it. But you must know this, you will find it. I know you will. Just as I did. Only a few years ago I thought I was a hopeless case, but now I'm blessed beyond my wildest imaginings."

"You deserve it." Charlotte kissed Rachel's cheek. "I'll see you later."

As Charlotte walked beneath the deck where they'd just been standing, she heard Rachel call out. "And don't forget! The quay at four tomorrow!"

Charlotte raised her thumb in silent acceptance before walking to her car, wishing she could bring her fierce, professional persona to her personal relationships. It seemed that, just like her father, she let her friends boss her around. Cam was right on that one point. She needed to stop. Just not yet.

~

THE NEXT DAY, Charlotte walked along the wooden jetty to the end of the quay. Small gift shops and cafés vied for passing tourists, but Charlotte's gaze was fixed on the end of the jetty where her date was waiting for her. She gave a low whistle and smoothed down her summer dress. This time, Rachel just might have got it right.

With blond hair trimmed neatly at the nape of the neck where it just touched a starched collar, her date was tall and well dressed. The shirt he wore was tailor made and fitted his body like a glove. As did the dress pants. She could see at a glance that they were expensive, designer clothes from their cut and cloth. They suited the wearer to a T. The man stood gazing out into the distance. She could see the square jaw and the side of his dark glasses. He stood as if he owned the place, like a movie star surveying his personal stretch of water and private yacht which bobbed in front, its pennant snapping in the breeze. Maybe it *was* his.

Suddenly someone called out and the man half-turned. He was even better looking from the side. He had the face of an... Charlotte faltered in her step. An Adonis, she said to herself, as she halted. Who else had she said that about?

Then the man turned further and waved at someone who was cruising past in a motorboat. They exchanged a few manly insults, laughed, and he turned to face her. Yep, it was definitely Cam Connelly.

He took off his sunglasses and, even though she knew it was him, there was a part of her which was still impressed. He looked so... so perfect. So different from his usual low-key self. His mouth split into a broad grin.

"Charlotte! You came!"

She shook her head. "I wouldn't have if I'd known it was you."

Annoyingly, he laughed. "That's why we decided not to tell you." He forced his features into a serious expression. "However, now that you know it's me, you're perfectly entitled to turn right around and walk back along the quay and return home. Absolutely. Entitled," he said with emphasis.

She opened her mouth to speak, but theatrically he raised a hand to stop her. "Before you say anything, I would just like to point out that I had a haircut especially for you. And that these"—he plucked at the shirt and pants—"have been bought for me by my lovely sister, Rachel, to tidy me up a bit. So," he said, putting his head to one side, "would you really like to see Rachel waste her money?"

He looked so comical standing there, a slight pout on his lips as he tried to turn her irritation to humor. But she refused to be taken in.

"You've both tricked me. You're as bad as each other." She bit her lip to stop herself from laughing and turned away, not wanting him to see the effect he was having on her.

"I'm sorry, Charlie," he said, obviously imagining her to be more upset than she was. "If you want me to go, I'll leave."

She closed her eyes as her smile broadened, her back still to him. Her shoulders quaked a little as she tried to keep in the laughter.

"We shouldn't have done this," he said, obviously mistaking her laughter for tears. "Don't blame Rachel. She knows how much I like you and she has this crazy idea that we'd be good together."

She turned to face him. "I'm not angry with Rachel. Do you want to know the only thing I'm upset about?"

He nodded, evidently relieved. "Yes, I do."

"That I suspect I'll enjoy my date with you, and that I'll suffer all the more because of it when you leave." She opened her arms and let them slap back against her thighs. "Cam, you'll be gone in a few short weeks. So what's the point?"

"I'll be here for Christmas Eve. There is that."

"True."

"And we could have a fun time during those few short weeks."

"There is that, too. But what you're missing is the risk."

He took a step toward her. "There's always a risk in everything we do. But," he said, his hands flexing if he were having to stop himself from reaching out to her, "there's also a risk in not doing something."

She swallowed. It was exactly what she'd been thinking. "We could miss out," she said.

He nodded. "Why don't we go ahead on the date I have planned and enjoy the day? Just enjoy each moment because that's all I can offer. Is that enough?"

She shouldn't, but she found herself nodding. "I guess so. If that's all that's on offer, it will have to be enough. A few days, maybe even a few weeks of fun, would be nice. And," she said, adding a lighter tone "it would get me out of a situation with my father."

"Ah, your father. I'm looking forward to meeting him," he said, stepping closer and offering his arm in an old-fashioned gesture. She slipped her hand through his arm and he brought it close and squeezed it against his side.

"That sounds slightly ominous," she said, as he led her along the side of the jetty. She still didn't know where they were going, but assumed it was an upmarket restaurant not far away.

He stopped walking and turned to her. "Ominous? No. But I am curious to meet the man who can make a grown woman quake."

"I don't quake!" she said, annoyed to be portrayed in any way less than strong.

"Well, he certainly undermines you."

"You will... well, you will be nice, won't you?"

He grinned. "I'm always nice." He looked over her shoulder. "Like now. I have considered your comfort." He gestured toward a boat, which was bobbing at the bottom of the jetty. "I have a blanket in case you're chilly out on the water, as well as a picnic put together by my sister. If I hadn't been so nice, I'd have packed the picnic basket myself."

She looked from the boat to him. "We're going out on the water?"

His face fell a little. "Yes, I thought it would make a change."

"Well, it certainly will for me. I've never been in a boat that small."

His face screwed up into an incredulous expression. "Never?"

She shook her head. "I've never been that comfortable on the water and, well"—she shrugged—"it never came up."

"Well, it has now. And I will make sure you're comfortable. You might want to slip off those shoes to begin with. I don't want you falling into the water. The rungs on the ladder are a bit slippery. Here, let me go first and then if you fall, you'll fall on me."

She laughed, but let him take a few steps before he reached back to hold her hand. He jumped down into the boat and kept it steady for her while helping her in. She squeaked as it gave a little wobble but sat down where he indicated and soon got used to the rocking and pitching as

Cam moved around the boat, unhooking the rope and settling down in front of the motor.

He grinned at her. "Ready?"

She nodded. "Ready."

The motor roared into life and Cam, with his shirt-sleeves rolled up and his expensive jacket now lying casually where he'd left it—draped over the picnic basket and at risk of becoming drenched with sea water—steered the boat directly across the harbor. Charlotte suddenly realized she hadn't a clue where they were headed.

"Where are we going?"

"Anchorage Bay."

It was a bay on the far side of the harbor. "I've never been that far along the coast."

"We're going just a little further than that, just past Cape Three Points Island."

Charlotte turned to one side so she could watch as they approached. She clamped her hand to her hair as the wind picked up the farther out to the middle of the harbor they reached. The hills were emerald green in the rich afternoon sun and the sea a brilliant deep blue. Everything seemed to sparkle with life. Everything seemed a little more vivid than it had when she'd woken up that morning.

She turned to look at Cam. He was in his element here. Outside on the water, or on the land, he wasn't a man for offices, no matter how he'd dressed today. She looked away to hide a smile, but the image of his tanned, handsome face, still filled her mind. His blue eyes were narrowed against the sunlight now. The sunglasses had also been discarded— another Rachel choice, Charlotte suspected. The funny thing was that he didn't look any different in his smart clothes. He had such a sense of power and uncompromising strength about him—not in terms of bulked-up muscle, but in his innate presence. He had *mana*, as Maori would say—presence, authority. And she never failed to react to it. He wore his clothes, they didn't wear him or seem to affect him in any way, shape or form. She wondered what in this world could shake his sense of self. Whatever it was, she hadn't seen it yet.

"Over there," he said, pointing to a patch of seemingly dense native trees above a small sandy cove. "That's where we're going."

"It looks wonderful. And remote," she added, as she looked around. Farmland, dotted with sheep, flowed all around the dark green patch of trees.

"Not too remote. My mate has a tree house amongst the trees. No power though. It's completely off the grid."

"I can't see a road."

"There isn't one. It's sea access only. Either that or a long hike over the hills."

She laughed, shaking her head. "None of my friends live off grid. They're all firmly plugged in."

"You should try it sometime. There's something very freeing about it."

She grunted. "You and your freedom."

She wished she could have retracted the words because he didn't fire back a quick response, but remained silent for a few moments.

"You still believe it, don't you?" he said.

"What?"

"That I live my life in a selfish pursuit of freedom."

"I'm sorry, I was angry. I should never have said such a thing. Forget it."

"But I can't forget it."

"Why?"

"Because you're right. In some ways, you're right. The other reason I can't forget it is that *you* said it, that *you* believe it."

"You're wrong. I don't believe it. Okay, I might have done

when I said it but I know the only selfish thing about you is that you don't stop working for something when you believe in it."

He was silent as he navigated the wash from a passing boat before steering the boat close to the far shore.

"Rachel says that you're like your mother in that way."

He eased the power from the motor and they slowed their pace as they passed a rocky promontory from which a flock of seabirds rose, protesting loudly that their isolation had been breached.

"Yes, I am. Mum made a stand every day of her life for what she believed in. And I try to, too. Yes, I move around a lot. I keep on moving, but I'm always true to my beliefs. I always make a stand and I don't move from that stand."

She nodded. "I know that now. I've seen you in action. But, you know, you say you and your mother shared the same beliefs."

He nodded, and she hesitated, wondering how she could challenge him on the one thing which she couldn't get out of her mind.

"And yet, surely, she was all about putting down roots—roots which you say you don't want."

He turned away as if she'd slapped him. She gathered her courage and carried on.

"It's almost as if you're afraid."

For a split second, his face tensed. Then he controlled himself and his expression relaxed into a faint glimmer of a smile. "You sure know how to get at a guy."

"Yeah, that's my secret power. It's why none of my relationships have lasted."

"If your straight-talking is enough to drive a man away, then I reckon you're better off without him."

She bit her lip. "I'm just wondering if my straight-talking has been enough to drive *you* away."

He didn't pause, only shook his head, and steered the boat up onto the steep, sandy beach. He jumped out, dragged it up further, and helped her out. But he didn't release her hand. Instead, he kissed it.

"Drive me away? You have to be kidding. Your straight-talking has only made me want you more."

She swallowed. "You want me?" she repeated, her body turning to jelly at the thought.

"I don't mean only physically—although believe me, I do —but I love talking to you. You interest me, engage me, challenge me. You—"

But she'd had enough talking. She rolled onto her tiptoes and pressed her lips to his, and kissed him like she'd been wanting to ever since she'd recognized him, standing at the end of the jetty.

"Hm," he said as she lowered herself once more. His hands cupped her face, holding her tenderly as he looked into her eyes. "You are something else, Charlotte. But I have to get something off my chest before we go any further. You're right. Your challenge to me, that I'm afraid is correct. I *am* afraid and I've been indulging that fear for years."

"What is it you're afraid of?" she asked, intrigued by his admission, despite a desperate desire to stop talking and continue kissing.

"Emotional pain," he said, typically succinct. "I'm terrified of a repeat of what happened when Mum died. We were so close, and I felt destroyed and empty when she passed away. I hadn't known she was so sick. Dad thought it best to keep it from us."

"So..." She paused, wondering whether to take it any further, but she had no choice. Cam had opened up to her like he never had before, not even to Rachel, who had often voiced her concern at Cam's keeping his emotions under such a tight rein. "You've avoided being close to anyone."

He nodded. "Until now."

She pressed her hand against his, which still cupped her cheek. "Cam, I…"

He pressed his finger to her lips. "I know, Charlotte, I know. I'm a bad risk. I'm not the kind of man you're looking for on your dating profile, that's for sure. But I'm here, now, and for the life of me, I can't pull away from you. You're all I think about, all I dream about."

"Kiss me," she said. Talking wouldn't get her anywhere because he was correct. They *were* wrong for each other. But at that moment, she didn't care.

He took her by the hand and led her away from the beach, leaving the things as they were, and walked up the steps to the small tree house which perched among the bush. The whole of the facade was glass. It looked like an enormous eye, staring without blinking across the water to Akaroa. When they got to the deck, which ran beneath the window, she turned and looked across the harbor. A lot had happened since they'd left the quay. She couldn't see her small cottage tucked away in the center of Akaroa, but she could see the rest of the town, including the cafés and shopping area, the houses piling up the hill. Among the oldest houses and most prominent were Flo's house along the beachfront, and Belendroit out to one side, remote and snug amidst the trees and the half-moon bay of Lantern Bay.

"You can see the entire world from here." She smiled and turned to him.

"I know. I'm looking at it right now." But his gaze hadn't moved away from her face and he kissed her again. Then, for a few heart-stopping moments, he searched his pockets before triumphantly holding up the house key.

They didn't make it further than the sitting room through which the sun streamed. The wide sofas covered with cushions overlooked only by the sea, the birds and the trees were the perfect place to make love. And that was all she wanted. That moment. With Cam.

8

*A*s morning broke around the tree house and the soft gray light of dawn entered the bedroom through the uncurtained windows, Charlotte looked at Cam who lay sleeping beside her. Charlotte didn't want their time here to end. Nestled amongst the trees, with no one else to complicate their lives, she felt she'd stepped outside of her life. She was outside time and outside her worries about the future. There was only her and Cam. Cam.

He looked even more beautiful asleep, because there was no tension around his mouth. There was no slight frown as he used his fierce intellect to resolve the world around him into something with which he could cope—something without emotion, something he could walk away from at any time before he could be hurt.

A wave of tenderness filled her, and she surrendered to the luxury of studying every detail of his face, impressing it into her mind. She wanted to remember everything about him forever. Finally, her gaze settled on his lips. A mouth that teased her with his clever tongue, both in what he said and other ways. She sucked in a ragged breath as she remembered the details of their night together, and his eyes flickered open.

He gave her a lazy smile, rolled on top of her, and kissed her.

"You're awake early," he said, his low, sexy voice rumbling through her body.

She moved her fingers down his back before coming to rest on his bottom. She felt the effect of her caress in other places.

"I have to go home and change before I get to work."

"But you're the boss, aren't you?" He shifted his hips a little. No distance at all, but suddenly her body was primed for action once more.

"Yes." Her breath hitched as he kissed her neck and lower.

"Then I reckon there's no hurry."

"And then there's the meeting at the marae." She half-whimpered the last word as she caressed his body, teasing him with her fingernails.

"Zane will understand if we're a little late." His voice was muffled as his lips continued to move down her body.

"What you don't seem to understand, Cam, is that I'm never late."

He stopped kissing her and looked at her with surprise. "You called me Cam… Charlotte."

"I did. And you called me Charlotte."

"Hm," he said, wriggling closer to her, his eyes ranging over her face as he raked his fingers through her hair, holding her face still before kissing her. "I guess that means we're finally accepting each other for who we are."

"I suppose so," she said, a little breathless now as she realized she'd be much later than she imagined for work. "And about being late."

"Hm?" he said, his voice muffled as he moved lower still.

"There's a first for everything," she said with a smile.

She felt him laugh against her sensitive skin.

FOUR HOURS LATER, and Charlotte still could not wipe the smile from her face as she drove up the drive to the welcoming embrace of Belendroit.

They had a last meeting at the marae before Christmas. Then there was a week's holiday before the New Year, after which Cam would leave. But she was determined not to think about that. She would do what everyone else did and live in the present. It had worked nicely for her over the past eighteen hours. In fact, she felt irrevocably changed in that short time. But she wouldn't think about that either. All she'd do was luxuriate in the pleasurable afterglow of loving Cam Connelly.

She got out of the car and looked around her for a few moments, breathing deeply of the place where Cam grew up. The flowers shifted in the sea breeze, creating ripples of orange, blue, and white beneath the trees. There was no sound escaping the house today and she could hear the lazy roll of the sea on the sand, and the cry of a heron as it took flight across the water. Then she turned to face the house. A lump rose in her throat.

It wasn't a perfect house. Like anything well-loved, it looked a little shabby around the edges. The garden was on the unkempt side, and some weatherboards needed sanding down and a good paint job. Charlotte knew that some of Jim's children noticed these things more than others, but Jim wouldn't allow them to change anything. He had a sentimental urge to keep things just as they were when his wife was alive. As she walked toward the front door, she could see evidence of this on the covered veranda. Shawls were casually strewn over the back of cane chairs, worn straw sun hats were layered on pegs, and knickknacks which, Cam had told her, his mother had acquired, lined the windowsill inside the house. Apparently she'd been like a magpie, spotting and collecting anything quirky which took her fancy.

She frowned as she approached the front door. It was closed. Last time she'd been there, it had been wide open. She knocked on the door. There was no answer. She knocked again and heard firm footsteps walking towards her.

Cam swung open the front door, reached for her, and kissed her passionately on the lips. Eventually he pulled away but kept a firm hold of her hands, as if he were worried she'd escape.

"It seems like an age since I've kissed you."

"An hour," she murmured against his mouth. But she, too, wished the house was empty and he could take her into one of the rooms and make love to her again.

"Hm," he said, "that's too long."

She could see which way his thoughts were progressing. She laughed against his neck, smelling him, loving the feel of him against her mouth.

"We're late already, and I'm sure Jim wouldn't think much of us disappearing into your bedroom."

Cam sighed and pulled away. "That's where you're wrong. I reckon Jim would be very pleased we've got together. He's been dropping hints about it ever since I arrived."

Charlotte was shocked. "I didn't know that."

"It's a wonder. My dad isn't known for his tact and diplomacy. Anyway"—he shot a look down the hall—"Dad doesn't seem to be himself today." He grimaced and looked uncharacteristically unsure. "I don't know what's going on."

Charlotte frowned and looked down the hall to the kitchen door, which was ajar. "I don't hear the usual jazz."

"No, he didn't turn it on today. Just came in and sat down, like he was exhausted."

"Jim? Exhausted?" Charlotte didn't like the sound of that.

She'd never seen him anything less than vitally alive and charismatic.

She followed Cam down the hall and, for a fleeting second as she entered the kitchen, she saw Jim as she'd never seen him before. His face wasn't animated, his cheeks drooped and his color was off. He looked a pale gray imitation of his usual self.

"Jim?" she said, half-questioning, half in greeting.

He instantly lifted his face and gave her his usual cheery smile. "Charlotte, my dear. How lovely to see you! Come in, come in, and have a cup of tea and a chat. Although," he said, with his usual twinkle in the eye, "I'm sure it's not me you've come to see."

She glanced at Cam, who grinned and turned to fetch his father a cup of tea.

"I'm afraid I can't stop. I've come to take Cam to a meeting at the marae. We're running a little late already."

"Ah," said Jim with another beaming smile. "That would be because you and Cam were having a romantic tryst across the water."

Her smile fell, and a blush bloomed in its place. She shot Cam an accusatory look, but he only shrugged and smiled and folded his arms while he leaned against the kitchen bench.

"Dad! You're embarrassing Charlotte."

Jim raised his busy white brows. "Am I, my dear? I'm so sorry. But there's really nothing to be embarrassed about. Love makes the world go around."

This time it was Cam who looked embarrassed. He cleared his throat and walked across the room to pick up his shirt, which he pulled on over his t-shirt.

"Now, for goodness' sake, Dad, while we're away, take it easy. You look like—"

"I'm fine, I'm fine," Jim interrupted, waving his hand.

"Don't you worry about me. You've got enough to worry about—whether you should stay or go."

Cam made a dismissive grunting sound. "I'm not worrying about that. *You* are. And I suggest you stop. You don't look well."

Charlotte decided it was time to change the subject before a full-on argument erupted.

"I think we should be going, Cam. Zane said we should be there at mid-day."

"The marae is only up the hill," said Cam, obviously concerned about his father.

Charlotte frowned. "Yes, but the road to it is around the bay. It takes at least a quarter of an hour to get there."

"It would if we were going by car."

"And that's what we are doing."

"No." He peered out the window. "It's a lovely day for a walk."

"Then why am I here? I thought you wanted a lift."

"I don't recall asking you for one."

"Maybe not. But when I suggested I pick you up, you didn't refuse."

Cam shrugged. "Maybe because I thought it would be nice to walk across the fields with you."

It seemed her blush refused to disappear. She looked at Jim, who returned her look with a big grin.

"I'm hardly dressed for it," she said. She really didn't want to arrive at a meeting looking anything less than professional.

"Between my wife and the girls, this house is full of women's things," said Jim with a smile.

Charlotte turned to him, and it was obvious that he was enjoying Cam's flirtation with her.

"Thank you, Jim, but I doubt there will be any shoes to fit me."

"Oh, I'm sure there will be. Cam, why don't you find something suitable while Charlotte and I step outside?"

Cam nodded and disappeared into a distant part of the house, leaving Charlotte and Jim alone.

With a bit of effort, Jim eased himself out of the chair, stood for a moment and then nodded as if he'd been checking to see if he'd fall. "Let's wait on the veranda, shall we? It's my favorite place in the world."

Charlotte wondered whether she should help Jim, but he shooed her hand away. They walked slowly along the hall before they entered the front room, opened the French doors and stepped outside onto the veranda.

Jim took a deep breath. "What a beautiful day!"

"It is." She walked over to the edge of the balcony, gripped the railing, and looked around. In front of her were the trees which hid the road. To the right was one wing of the house, curving around in a protective shield, and to the other she could see the sea of Lantern Bay. She sighed and felt the remaining tension slip away. She turned her back to the view and looked at Jim. He'd sat down and was surveying her with a narrowed gaze, quietly and contemplatively. But, for some reason, it didn't make her feel uncomfortable.

"You look right here," he said at last. "As if you belong."

Charlotte was startled, not least because she *felt* right here. She shrugged awkwardly. "I guess I feel right in Akaroa." She decided to interpret his words more broadly.

"No, what I mean is that you look right *here* at Belendroit. There's something about you. I'd always thought you looked a little lost. But here, you look as if you've been found."

She smiled. "That, Jim, is an extremely fanciful notion."

But he didn't return her smile. "I don't know about fanciful, but the older I get, I sometimes think, the more truly I see things. It's as if the things that don't matter fall away, leaving only the things that do. I see you clearly, Charlotte. Just as I see my son, clearly."

Her smile faltered. "And what do you see?"

"I see a couple who were meant to be together."

She shook her head. "I don't believe in fate. I believe in common sense, shared interests, compatible personalities. There's nothing beyond that."

He gave a gentle laugh. "You may have thought that once, but now?" He shook his head. "I doubt it. There's something more than that, something extra, something special, and you know it when you see it. Deep down, Charlotte, you know it."

She swallowed, trying to resist believing him. But knowing he spoke the truth. She tried to speak, but shook her head instead.

"And all you have to do is accept what your heart already knows. You've found us here, in this place, and Belendroit is yours to love. As is my son, if you'll have him."

She was saved from responding by Cam, who held up two luridly-colored training shoes. "Judging by the color, I think these must belong to Amber. But they're your size."

Thankful for the interruption, Charlotte slipped off her high-heeled court shoes. She loved shoes, particularly ultra feminine ones with high heels. She blinked as she took hold of Amber's old shoes. They had to be the ugliest things she'd ever seen, but she could hardly ask if there was any other choice.

Gritting her teeth, she pushed her feet into the trainers, which made her feet look twice their size. She shook her head at their ugliness and in disbelief because they were comfortable. Really comfortable. She tied the fluoro pink and green laces in a decisive double knot and nodded at Cam.

"Okay, a walk it is."

"I promise you," he said, in that voice which could do things to her on its own, "you won't regret it."

Their gazes tangled for a moment, and Charlotte was sure that he was quite wrong. She would most definitely regret it. Later. Not yet.

He grinned at her reaction and went and kissed his father on the head. Jim patted Cam's arm. Charlotte marveled at how demonstrative their relationship was compared to her own chilly and formal one with her father.

She said her goodbyes, and they walked outside.

"Are you worried about Jim?"

Cam nodded. "Something's going on and he's not telling anyone."

"I can understand that. I think I'd be like that. Jim obviously doesn't want to worry anyone."

"He's worrying us more by not telling us." He sighed as they crossed the road and entered a field along the side of which was a path which would take them up and over the hill to the valley beyond. "Anyway, I'd rather talk about you. I reckon those shoes look cute on you." He allowed his gaze to lazily track up her legs. She swore she felt it as if he were dragging a fingertip along her calf. Desire flickered inside her.

"Are you flirting with me, Cam Connelly?" she said with a sideways glance, before ducking under some overhanging trees which brushed her cheek.

"Flirting?" He shrugged. "Maybe a little. I can't seem to help myself when I'm around you."

"Well, you *should* help yourself. You should control it because (a) it's embarrassing and (b) there's no point."

"Why isn't there a point?"

"Because (a) you're leaving in a few weeks and..." She trailed off, forgetting her train of thought as he took a few steps forward, and raised his hand to her face, his fingers giving her cheek a quick caress. She gasped, wondering what he was going to do, all thought of remonstrating forgotten. His smile dropped a little, and he frowned as he plucked a stray twig from her hair. She released her breath, but he didn't move away. He was so close that she could feel his warm breath on her face, could smell the freshly ironed smell of his shirt and something more, something male and mouth-watering. His lips opened, and she thought he was about to kiss her.

"I love the way you speak in bullet points," he said instead. "It's so precise and to the point. Your thoughts are as clear as your emotions are complicated. Intriguing," he said, shifting a little nearer. She couldn't help herself and lifted her face to his, wanting him with every fiber of her being. He granted her unspoken wish and kissed her, his hands coming around her face and holding her as if she were the most precious thing in the world. When he pulled away, she felt she could fall into the deep blue of his eyes, like into a warm sea.

"Cam, we can't go on like this. Indulging ourselves. You'll be leaving soon, and I..."

"Won't be leaving," he finished her sentence. "I know. But," he said, looking around. "It's a fine morning. Let's forget that for today."

She knew he was correct and she also knew she wanted, above all else, to forget, so they carried on up the field until they reach the top of the hill. From there, they looked down the valley at the Maori settlement. Zane and Rachel lived in their glorious homestead overlooking the valley, while most of the other houses were grouped around the traditional meeting house which took centre stage in the middle of the valley. Outside the meeting house, people were waiting for them.

Cam waved, and Zane waved back. Cam extended his hand to her, and she took it. She'd forget about the future for as long as she could. But she knew, at some point, they'd both have to face reality and she couldn't bear to imagine what that reality would look, or feel, like.

AT THE END of the morning, after the formal discussions were over and agreement had been reached over the project by everyone concerned, Zane took them both to his house, high on the hill, where Rachel was testing some recipes. Wonderful fragrances wafted down from the kitchen, making Charlotte's mouth water.

Rachel walked out from the kitchen, her hands on her hips, and looked from Charlotte to Cam before a wide grin spread over her face.

"Your date went okay, then?"

"You could have told me," said Charlotte, only half-reproachfully. How could she be cross with Rachel for setting her up for one of the most wonderful evenings and nights of her life?

Rachel kissed Charlotte on the cheek. "If I'd told you, would you have gone?"

Charlotte shrugged. "I don't know."

"Then I'm glad I didn't." Rachel cocked her head to one side and surveyed Charlotte. "Because *you* look a different woman."

Charlotte sighed and shook her head. "You're as bad as your father."

"Why? What did he say?"

"Just that..." But the thought of repeating what Jim had said about fate and that she and Cam were meant for each other didn't appeal.

"Yes, well, no need to go into details. I can guess. Dad and I are pretty similar. We think the same things. Like about you two." She glanced at Cam.

"There's not much point in doing anything other than thinking. Cam is intent on leaving in the New Year."

"Not if I've got anything to do with it." Rachel nodded her head to where Zane and Cam were chatting outside. "I've set Zane onto it. Zane never fails at anything."

CAM WONDERED if his whole family was in on a conspiracy to keep him in New Zealand, specifically in Akaroa, even more specifically at Belendroit. Even Zane hadn't dwelled on the project he purportedly wanted to discuss. But had, instead, dived straight into a discussion about Cam's personal life, without bothering with any preliminaries. It didn't take a genius to see that Zane was acting under orders. Cam glanced at Rachel, who was in deep conversation with Charlotte. Families!

"What have you got against staying?" asked Zane, standing tall, one hand cradling a beer, the other stuffed into his trouser pocket. He was one formidable man and Cam could imagine exactly how formidable he'd been when he'd played rugby for the All Blacks. His opponents hadn't stood a chance.

"Not you, too," Cam groaned. "How about cutting me some slack?"

Zane followed Cam's glance at Rachel. "No way, mate. I've got to report back to Rachel and she'll be expecting progress on her 'get my brother to stay in New Zealand' scheme."

Cam grinned. Rachel could also have halted an army with her beauty and charm. "And that is exactly why I want to leave. Too much family stuff going on for my liking. I don't know how you cope with it all."

Zane frowned. "That's why I returned. My life with the All Blacks wasn't real. This is. I couldn't cope without having family around. I reckon you've got it back to front, mate. Shame, too, because you're the perfect person to lead the Lake Waitahi project."

"No way. I'm out of here in the New Year."

Zane's face lightened, and he grunted in amusement. "A woman, is it?"

Cam nodded, knowing that Zane had got it half right. Zane assumed he had a woman in England he was going to. Zane had no idea that it was a woman here, a woman who threatened his heart like no one had ever done before, that he was running from. Flo was right. He was scared. And with good reason. Charlotte was someone special, someone who he couldn't commit to because he couldn't commit to anything or anybody.

"No, mate, there's no way I'm staying."

"But you seem happy."

Cam shrugged. "Sure, it's nice. I…" He trailed off. How could he explain everything in his heart to Zane? It was contradictory, it was confusing, it was suicide. "I don't know. It's hard to explain."

"Give me something to tell Rachel, for goodness' sake."

"Tell her…" He took a slug of beer. "Tell my sister that I can sort my own life out."

Zane just laughed. "Yeah, right. That's what she's afraid of."

At that moment, Rachel and Charlotte joined them on the deck with some food and drinks. The hours slipped away and Cam soon forgot about Zane's interrogation as he enjoyed Charlotte's company. Things were different between them since they'd spent the night together and it must have shown, because Rachel treated them as if they were a couple.

"So what plans have you two got tonight?" asked Rachel. "Would you like to stay for dinner?"

Cam felt a little uncomfortable. As much as he enjoyed

being with Charlotte, the thought of being regarded as part of a couple unnerved him. Charlotte's smile dropped as if she'd read Cam's thoughts. She opened her mouth to speak but, whatever Charlotte was about to say was interrupted by the growing sound of an ambulance siren.

Rachel's brow furrowed. "That's strange. It's not coming from the direction of Akaroa. It's..." She looked up, suddenly startled, to Cam, who was one step ahead of her.

"It's coming from Belendroit," he said. He stood up and checked his phone and rang Jim's number. But there was no answer.

"I'll drive you across the paddock in the four-wheel drive. It'll be quicker," said Zane.

All four of them piled into the car and bumped across the rough paddock. Cam jumped out and opened the gate and they joined the road which led to Belendroit. They arrived there just as the ambulance men appeared, carrying out a stretcher from the front door.

Cam rushed up to them and saw Jim, his face ghostly gray.

"What the hell's happened?"

"I collapsed," said Jim faintly. "No need to make a fuss."

"You didn't call me. You said you'd call if you needed me."

"I didn't need you," said Jim, lying down again, looking exhausted. He closed his eyes.

"He needed us," said the ambulance man. "And we need to get Jim to the hospital quickly. Would you like to travel with us?"

Cam didn't need asking twice. As the van doors were closed behind them, he held his father's hands, still in shock. Because, out of all the scenarios in the world, losing his father had never featured in any of them.

*a*s the evening turned into night more of the Connelly family arrived at the hospital, until they'd taken over most of the waiting room. Every time another of Cam's siblings entered the room, he'd give them the same reply.

"No change."

It had been decided that only Gabe should stay with Jim, while he underwent a barrage of tests to find out why he'd collapsed. He was a doctor and so more likely to understand the situation and, most importantly, he was able to stay calm, unlike any of the others, excluding Cam. Gabe had told them early on that the records showed Jim had cancer and had been procrastinating over the treatment. He hadn't told anybody. The concern was that the cancer had spread and had caused Jim to collapse. But they wouldn't know until all the test results were returned.

Now and then Gabe came through to the waiting room to update them, but there hadn't been any change and the doctors didn't expect any for some time. The minutes ticked by so slowly that Cam had the uncanny feeling that he was suspended in time. It gave him too much time in which to think, too much time in which to *feel*. But there was one good thing about having a family who wore their hearts on their sleeves—they needed him to be strong. It gave him something to cling to, something to stop the slide into grief which threatened him.

He looked around the clinical waiting room. Rachel lay asleep, stretched out across the chairs, her head in Zane's lap. Zane sat upright, self-contained and fast asleep. Amber sat white-faced, with tear-stained cheeks, refusing to leave the hospital, no matter what David, her husband, said. He'd under-estimated his little sister. For all her eccentricities, she was as strong and as staunch as the best of them when it came to her family.

Beside Amber sat Rob, who watched Etta pace up and down the floor. Etta had grown up not knowing Jim was her grandfather, but ever since she'd been reunited with Rachel, her birth mother, she and Jim had formed a strong bond and she, too, refused to leave. Cam sighed. He knew the hospital wouldn't be best pleased with yet more Connellys arriving. Lizzi and Pete and Max and Laura were expected any time. They'd all dropped everything to be with Jim. He was the fulcrum of their family, the patriarch who none of them could ever imagine being without. He was loud, charismatic, occasionally outrageous, and absolutely adored by all of them.

Charlotte suddenly shifted in her sleep, her head nestled against his shoulder. His arm had gone to sleep, but he didn't want to move it in case he woke her. Instead, he kissed her hair, which was no longer perfect but tumbled around her shoulders. She smelled of lemony shampoo and the vestiges of expensive perfume. Her fragrance was uniquely her. He closed his eyes and inhaled her once more, suddenly realizing he needed her presence as much as he needed air to breathe. She was a part of him now. He opened his eyes with a start, and once more stared at the clock, as if for reassurance. It was as if his world had tilted off its axis. How could he allow someone to be a part of him? He had no control over that. Sweat prickled his forehead, and he wiped it roughly, disturbing her.

She moaned lightly and turned to him. "Are you okay?"

"Sure," he said, taking the opportunity to withdraw his arm. He leaned forward, rested his arms on his thighs and rubbed his scratchy eyes. But he'd lied. He wasn't okay. He was fighting emotion with all his might. He didn't want it—not a bit of it. It had been proved he couldn't cope with emotion when his mother had died. There was only one way he could live his life, and that was without it.

"Sure," he repeated, jumping up. That was better. He needed to be separate from her. No physical contact. He could do this. He could withdraw. Already the pain of seeing his father's face an unrecognizable mask, was fading. He filled a cup with water. "Would you like one?" he asked, eventually looking at her.

She looked hurt. He hadn't said anything to hurt her, but she was hurt anyway. It proved that he'd let things progress too far. He'd wanted flirtation. He'd wanted her to realize how special she was. What he hadn't wanted was to form a connection with her. But it seemed he'd done exactly that.

He looked back at the water, focusing on making sure it didn't spill over. He felt an overwhelming need for control, as if not only his, but his father's life, depended on it. He drank back the over-chilled water, tossed his cup in the bin and returned to his seat beside Charlotte, who looked at him with concern, as if sensing his thoughts. But before she could speak, there was a rush of cool air in the overheated waiting room as the doors opened and Max and Lizzi rushed through.

"Where is he?" asked Max, walking up to the end of the corridor and looking around. Trust his eldest brother, thought Cam. Max thought he could walk right on into the hospital, up to his father's bed, and make things right. "How is he?"

When Cam had left Akaroa, Max and his father hadn't been the best of friends. Cam had been too young to know exactly what was going on but, whatever it was, that rift had now healed and Max was extremely close to Jim.

"Gabe is with him."

"Gabe? Right, right," said Max, agitatedly, raking his fingers through his hair. "So, when can I see him?"

"Not until we're allowed to. Gabe will tell us when."

"Why not now? What the hell is going on that I can't see my own father?" Max's eyes were bright with anger, masking his fear. By the way he paced the small space, Cam could see that adrenalin raged through his body.

Cam reached out and placed a hand on Max's shoulder. "Hey, Max, it's difficult for us all. You need to calm down."

Max flung away his hand and turned on Cam, his eyes blazing.

"Calm? Like you, you mean?" said Max, eyeing his brother with irritation.

Cam wasn't about to tell Max that his calm was hard won and he refused to rise to the bait. "Exactly."

Max made a scoffing sound and turned away. Rachel shot them a worried look. Cam understood Max was upset and angry—all the things he, himself, avoided—and that Max was taking it out on him, the nearest person Max felt could take it. But Cam wasn't so sure he *could* take it. He felt a burst of anger, which he was only barely able to control. He gritted his teeth and tried to contain his anger, but then Max made another derisive sound. Cam was hanging on by a thread now.

Max turned to Cam and looked at him and shook his head. "How can you stand there so placidly, as if you have no feelings for anyone? Hey? You always have that cold, intellectual thing going on. It's like you're a robot or something."

Cam's mind continued to operate logically, rationally, calmly. But only just. His heart pounded, and it took all his willpower not to reveal his inner fears and emotions. While he battled to suppress the chaos which lurked only skin deep, he was aware of Charlotte jumping up, wanting to defend him. He placed a hand on her arm.

He turned to Max. "I'm calm because that's the way I am. It doesn't mean I don't have feelings."

"You think?" asked Max, who didn't appear to have a calm bone in his body. Max walked up to Cam, his grief and fears fueling his anger. "Show me then."

Charlotte gasped and pushed away Cam's hand.

"For goodness' sake! Of course Cam cares." Charlotte looked from Max to Cam and then back to Max with blazing eyes, indignation rolling off her in waves. "How can you say he doesn't?"

Cam balled his hands into fists, desperately trying to keep control, ignoring Charlotte, focused only on Max. "I don't need to show you anything." He looked Max up and down, remembering all the times his firebrand brother had returned home with a black eye and fierce determination.

Max made a derisive sound. "I don't believe anything gets to you."

Max poked Cam in the chest, and then the flood of emotion which he'd been holding back for so long was released. With one quick movement, he swung his fist toward Max's face. With an even quicker motion, Gabe, who had walked out of the doctor's area unnoticed, grabbed Cam's hand before it could connect.

Gabe swore. Both Max and Cam looked at him. Cam wasn't sure whether Gabe coming between them, or his swearing, was more remarkable. His sunny-tempered brother never got into fights and he'd never heard him swear.

"What the hell? Our father is sick in there and all you two idiots can think of doing is fighting?" Gabe pushed between them to get to the coffee machine.

Max looked away, abashed, and Cam stepped back and shook his head.

"You're right," said Cam. "Grief makes us do crazy things. Right, Max?"

"Right," said Max, offering his hand to Cam. It seemed a ridiculously formal thing to do and incongruous given where they were, but Cam took the hand, shook it. For a moment he imagined hugging his brother, something he hadn't done since they were children, but the moment passed. Instead, he turned to Gabe.

"Any news about Dad?"

Gabe stopped fiddling with the coffee machine settings for a moment before leaning against the machine and eyeing each of his siblings with a grim expression. Cam's heart sank. "As I said before, Dad's got cancer. That's what all the hospital visits were about. He told me they were routine, and I believed him."

Rachel put her arm around Gabe. "Dad can be pretty convincing. He just didn't want us to worry."

Gabe blinked, staring at the coffee machine. "Well, I'm worrying now." He pushed himself away and turned to face his family. "I'm waiting to hear if the cancer has spread. But they can't figure out what caused his collapse. It might be something straightforward, or it might not. In a worst-case scenario, he's going to need twenty-four-hour care and the only place he's going to get that is in a facility."

"Facility?" asked Amber, through cracked lips. She'd been quiet through the whole time they'd been in the hospital, but now her reddened eyes were blazing. "What do you mean, a facility?"

Gabe's gaze softened as it rested on Amber. David, her husband, had his arm firmly around her and it looked that it was only this which was keeping her from falling over.

"He'll need help to move around, help with everyday things for a little while, especially during treatment. Help which we can't give him."

"I can," said Amber, her voice stronger and defiant now. She turned to David. "We can, can't we, David?"

David frowned and looked at Gabe, who shook his head, before turning back to Amber. "Of course, we're going to do everything in our power to look after Jim. But you're pregnant, my darling. You can't provide twenty-four-hour care for your father. It's just not possible. And you have the café, too."

Amber's loud, keening wail filled the air, penetrating each of them, driving home the grief that their world had just been turned upside down. Amber's tears flowed down her cheeks as she turned and buried her face in David's chest. He folded her into him with such loving care that Cam could see that, despite how different the couple appeared, they were completely in love. He let his aching head fall back against the wall, and he stared dry-eyed and brittle with fear at the ceiling.

"Zane and I can be there for him," said Rachel.

"Flo and I will do our bit," said Rob.

"And me," said Etta.

"Between us all, we should be able to cover it," said Rob.

All eyes turned to Gabe who, as a doctor, was the only

one with the experience to know for sure. He shook his head. "It's too hard when you're emotionally involved. And with the best will in the world, you couldn't cope—none of you are medically trained."

"What about Cam?" said Amber. "You're living at Belen-droit, Cam. You could care for Dad."

"Cam's leaving in a few weeks," said Rachel, before Cam could respond. "We need a long-term plan for Dad."

But Amber's pleading eyes hadn't left Cam's face. Even while the rest of the family continued talking, continued to come up with plans that would ensure their father could live in the home he loved and with the people he knew.

"Cam," said Charlotte. With relief, he broke Amber's gaze and turned to Charlotte. "Let's go outside and get some air."

"Sure."

Outside, the sky was dark, and the stars were eclipsed by the city lights. But the air smelled good. Instinctively, they began walking out of the car park toward the dark shapes of the trees which lined the park.

"You feeling okay?" he asked, as they sat down on a park bench.

"Yes, I'm fine. It's you I'm worried about," she said. He took hold of her hands and tucked them under his jacket to keep warm.

He frowned. He really didn't want to talk about himself. "I'm fine."

"No, you're not," she said. "You might fool everybody else, Cam Connelly, but you can't fool me. You're nowhere near fine. Max is way off the mark when he thinks you're without emotions. I know you have them. I know you probably feel more than anyone else I know. That's why you have no choice but to keep those feelings under tight control. Unless you controlled them, you run the risk of being hurt. But Cam, isn't it worth taking a chance on opening up your heart? Maybe, just maybe, it might not be as bad as you fear."

Cam ground his teeth. He knew she spoke the truth. But he still didn't dare risk it. He hadn't exposed his emotions for years and had no idea what chaos would ensue if he took the lid off them.

"It's manageable," he said simply. "Life is manageable without emotions."

He nearly cracked as her eyes roamed his face. They were so full of tenderness. But he couldn't break down. That way lay madness.

"Is that all you want?" she asked, her voice cracking. "A manageable life?"

A lump rose into his throat and refused to move. He swallowed once, twice, felt the pricking of tears behind his eyes. What the hell?

"You must want more than that?" she urged, her hands now gripping the soft stuff of his shirt, as if she were trying to hang on to him. "You *must*."

He gave one sharp shake of the head. It was all he could manage. It was more of a reflexive jerk than a negation.

"Cam." His name emerged from her lips like a moan. "Please, don't do this to me, and don't do it to yourself."

He pressed his hands against hers, pushing their warmth into his chest, into his heart, which was pounding with a ferocity which she must feel. "Charlotte," he half-whispered, wondering himself what he was going to say next.

"I'm breaking up inside," she said with a sob. "I've found you, the person I want to be with, but you refuse to let me in."

He gripped her hands more tightly still. "But what if you don't like what you see when I let you in? Hey? Have you thought of that? Maybe the me you think you see isn't there.

Maybe I'm exactly as my brother Max describes me—shallow and cold."

She shook her head, and a tear trickled down her cheek. "You're not. I know you're not." She raised her hand, and he noticed it was shaking as she tenderly drew her fingers down his cheek. He took it in his hand and brought it to his lips and kissed her fingers. "It's hard, I know it's hard. Seeing your father so helpless. But it's still possible that Jim will recover and lead a normal life. Surely you want to be around when he does?"

Every word she spoke was true. He wasn't cold or shallow. His emotions ran deep and hot. That was why he'd had no choice but to cauterize them, if he were to live a normal, rational life. The kind of life which his brain told him he *should* live. And, yes, he wanted to be with his father, wanted to be home, with his family around him. But that meant there would be no moving on when things became hard.

"I don't know if I can do it." He felt something warm and wet trickle down his heated cheek. He brushed it away. He never cried.

"You can. With me by your side. I'll help you every step of the way. It won't be easy, but I believe what we have will be enough to see us through. I love you, Cam. I've been fighting it, but I love you."

"I can't do love."

"I think you've just done it."

She clasped his face between her hands and kissed him as if her life depended on it. It was as if she'd unlocked the key to his emotions and he kissed her back so passionately that for a moment he didn't know where he was when at last they fell apart. She held on to him as the tears, which had at first rolled silently down his cheeks, turned into quiet sobs and she continued to hold on to him as he shook and he felt himself crack inside, and the emotion pour out. He felt as if he were crying for everything that had happened in his life, for which he'd never grieved, and he wondered if it would ever end.

But it did. She kissed his wet cheeks and then his mouth, so tenderly that his newly awakened heart nearly made him cry again. But she pulled away and gripped both his hands in hers.

"We should go back, Cam. But this time, don't hide your emotions. It doesn't make you weak. In fact, I believe it will only make you stronger."

He sighed and swept his thumbs over her cheeks. "You are one wise woman."

She grunted dismissively. "I wouldn't go that far." They took a few steps and then she stopped. "Although, maybe you're right. Maybe with loving someone comes wisdom."

There was that word again. It seemed to haunt him and it still made him feel unsure and want to run a mile. But Charlotte was definitely right about one thing. It was time to face up to his life—the whole of it—and take responsibility for those he loved.

Hand in hand, they walked back into the hospital room. Everyone looked up as they entered the room. Cam realized it was probably to do with the fact that he and Charlotte were holding hands, but he didn't release hers.

"Amber's right," said Cam. "I'm the obvious choice to stay at Belendroit and look after Dad. I did some first responder work in London years ago. I may not be a trained nurse or doctor, but I know first aid. And I'm strong. I can look after him at Belendroit."

Amber came running over, flinging herself into his arms, and held on to him. "You are a darling. But you missed the news! There's no need now. While you were outside, Gabe told us it looks like the cancer hasn't spread and that the collapse was caused by low blood pressure. He doesn't need twenty-four-hour care."

Charlotte looked at him with both relief and fear. He looked away because he understood what she was afraid of. He'd said he'd stay because his father needed him. But he didn't need him now, did he?

He looked around at the relief and tears, and hugs which his siblings were giving each other. They'd been given a reprieve. Jim wasn't dying. His cancer hadn't spread, his treatment would be straightforward and the prognosis was good. He could return to Belendroit to pick up the threads of his life once more. But where did that leave him?

"Cam?" asked Charlotte softly.

He turned to her. They stood, unmoving, in the room, the only ones still and silent, not touching each other.

"Yes?"

"You know what I want to know. Will you still stay, Cam?" she asked. "Will you still stay?" she repeated, her voice ragged. He wished he could lie. It would make things so much simpler. But he couldn't avoid her gaze. He shook his head and her face winced in pain.

"I don't know," he said, taking a step away from her. He couldn't bear to see her like that. He sucked in a deep breath and closed his eyes. He didn't need to see Charlotte. She filled his head with her beauty and longing—a longing for someone who he wasn't sure was him. "I'm sorry, but I just don't know." The catch in her breath made him wince. His words had wounded her. If he'd turned and struck her, he knew it wouldn't have hurt as much as his words had.

"Then you'd better go." Her voice was hoarse, but it wasn't trembling. Not his Charlotte. She was strong. And she was better off without him. He not only wanted to leave for himself, he needed to leave for her.

He took one step in front of the other and kept on walking, out of the hospital, away from Charlotte and his family, with no clue what he was walking toward. He only knew that he was a loner—always had been and always would be—and to inflict that on such a caring, wonderful woman wasn't fair. He'd never be enough for her. And he wasn't the man his family thought he was.

10

*H*ow could the world carry on as normal when her life had just been turned upside down?

The sun continued to shine and she could hear children playing in the neighboring park while Charlotte steadied the ladder for Etta, who had one foot on the top and the other dangerously balanced on Charlotte's fence. How could he be so close to her one minute, opening up to her just as she'd imagined him doing, only to walk away again? The man was intolerable.

The memory of Cam walking away, refusing to look her in the eye after he'd done such an extreme about face, would not leave her mind. She thought it would be forever engraved there. Cam would stay for his father, but he wouldn't stay for her, nor for himself. It was clear how little he really felt for her.

And she was angry at herself for letting her feelings run out of control. She'd make sure *that* wouldn't happen again. Hell would have to freeze over before she spent any more time with him.

"Can you pass me the tinsel," called Etta, stretching out her hand.

But Charlotte didn't notice. All she could hear was Cam's voice and all she could feel was utter indignation. His brother was right. Cam *was* cold, distant, and would never change.

"The tinsel, Charlotte!" called Etta more loudly.

But not even this pierced Charlotte's consciousness. It was the bauble which Etta threw at her and which bounced off her head which made her look up.

Charlotte clamped her hand to her head and looked at Etta in disbelief. "What are you doing?"

"I'm trying to get your attention. I need more tinsel, Charlotte. Cam said you wanted this place looking Christmas-y for your dad, and that's what I'm trying to do. I have to leave in ten minutes. But we'll all be back to finish off later."

"I appreciate it, Etta. I'm hopeless with this sort of thing."

"Yeah, that's what Cam said."

"Hm!" grunted Charlotte, her pride ruffled. It was one thing for her to admit defeat when it came to crafty things, quite another for the man she loved to agree with her.

Etta must have taken Charlotte's grunt for annoyance that she had to leave. "After this, I've got Belendroit to do. I told Grandad I'd have it all ready before the carol singers arrive to practice. You are coming, aren't you?"

"I'm not sure."

Charlotte held the ladder with one hand while she picked up some tinsel and passed it to Etta. She didn't want to see Cam in the middle of his happy family, still refusing to accept he was a part of it. Besides, she felt like a fool for opening her heart to him, only to have him walk away.

"Grandad especially asked if you were coming."

"He did?"

"Yes, he did."

But Etta didn't meet Charlotte's eye, and she wasn't so sure Etta didn't have the Connelly trick of twisting the truth to get something she wanted. She narrowed her gaze, but Etta focused on the decorations. Etta fixed the tinsel into place and met Charlotte's gaze.

"What?" asked Etta, direct as ever. "Don't you like it?"

"I love it. It's just what you said about me coming to Belendroit. I'm not sure."

Etta sighed and jumped down from the ladder, rolling her eyes. "You don't have to be sure. You're not accepting some great honor or making a life decision. It's just a carol practice and food."

Put like that, Charlotte felt a little silly. She gave Etta a weak smile.

"Okay, I'll come."

"Good." Etta stood back and surveyed her handiwork. "That should be enough to do the top of the deck. 'Deck the hall with boughs of holly' and all that crap."

Charlotte was used to Etta and respected her for her powerful sense of self. You knew where you were with Etta, unlike others of her family, Charlotte thought grimly. "I thought you were into Christmas."

"Well," said Etta, grunting as she pinned the remaining holly around the deck. "I kind of like the partying. But I'm not so bothered about the rest." She looked at her handiwork. "But the family love it and Grandad, too. So…" She shrugged.

The family, thought Charlotte. Between her Maori heritage and the Connellys, Etta was always going to be big on family. But this morning, family was the last thing Charlotte wanted to hear about.

Etta crossed her arms and inspected her handiwork. "It's a start."

"You've done a great job," said Charlotte.

Etta pulled a face and turned to look at Charlotte. "But it's not the Christmas card you want yet. Not to worry, Cam and I will sort that out. We'll come around tomorrow."

Charlotte panicked at the thought. "Honestly, it's fine. It's..." She looked up the half-finished house and couldn't find the words to finish her sentence.

"It's not finished, is what it is. But it will be. I'll see you later," said Etta, picking up her army surplus bag and a black jersey which had seen better days, and walked up the garden path to the gate.

"Sure. And thanks for everything."

"No problem. Oh," said Etta, turning and walking backwards for a few steps while she spoke to Charlotte. "Uncle Cam told me to tell you he'd see you later. You were right. It wasn't only Grandad who wanted you to come. Uncle Cam told me I had to do whatever it takes to make sure you came. And, knowing you, I thought it might take a bit of honesty." She took a bite of an apple she'd plucked from her bag, let herself out of the gate and jogged away, leaving Charlotte standing under flashing lights with her mouth open.

Cam wanted her to go? She couldn't believe it. Why, for goodness' sake? He'd made it clear that the only future he could see was one without her. She grunted in frustration at the man who provoked such extreme emotions in her. She'd go to Belendroit. She'd see Cam, and she'd make damn sure that he'd see he had no effect on her whatsoever. He meant nothing to her. She blinked to stop the pricking at the back of her eyes. Nothing, she insisted firmly.

"AND WHY ON earth you should just walk away like that, Cam," blazed the usually cheerful Amber, "is beyond me."

Cam contented himself with a glare at his annoying little

sister and turned his attention back to the cake which Rachel had brought around earlier. Belendroit certainly was never short of good baking.

"It's not beyond *me*," said Jim, tucked under a blanket—despite his desperate remonstrances that he was too hot—and made to rest on a sofa, which he'd always ignored before. Now, its crocheted and aged embroidered cushions, which had been plumped by his wife years before, were tenderly tucked under his back and neck. He didn't dare move, thought Cam with a smile. Not now Amber had turned into such a vigilant nurse, determined not to let her father down on her watch.

Jim flourished his hand at Cam. "The boy's scared. There's no big mystery there." Jim took a slurp of his tea before settling back to his cryptic crossword. Cam and Amber looked at each other.

"Will you two stop talking about me as if I'm not here?" he said calmly.

Jim simply shot him a quizzical look from under his white, bushy eyebrows while Amber ignored him.

"Cam? Are you scared?" Amber's tone was softer now, as if she were trying to soothe a toddler. Even though Amber's babies were only just beginning to show, her hand often caressed them, cupping her stomach as if reassuring the babies that all would be well. And her maternal instinct extended beyond her stomach to everyone around her—especially her family. David had said he couldn't wait for the birth, so she'd stop mothering him. But, while Amber's tone might be softer, her eyes defied avoiding. There was no way he could lie to her.

He did weird things with his lips to avoid a direct answer.

"Cam," she said in a lower warning tone.

"Maybe," he said, picking up some cups to take into the

kitchen. He walked away but heard Amber following him. It didn't look as if he'd escape this one.

She closed the door behind her so Jim couldn't hear their conversation.

"Maybe? Dad's right, isn't he? You're terrified."

He glared at her as he set down the dishes. "You're going too far."

"Am I?" she said, as she stalked over to him and walked around him as if he were prey. "I don't think I'm going far enough!"

His eyes shot open. What had happened to his sweet little sister? Pregnancy was turning her into some goddess-type creature of supernatural strength.

"In fact," she said, hands on hips, directly in front of him, so he had no option but to face her. "I think it's about time we had some straight words. Sit down."

He found himself sitting down, but she didn't. She leaned over him.

"You can run, but you can't hide."

"What?"

Amber still had the unique ability of any of his family to confuse him with her lack of logic.

"From love. Which, I take it, is exactly what you've been doing. Running, so you can't feel anything—good or bad. It'll get you in the end, Cam, so you may as well accept it. You have a heart for love—anyone can see that—so you might as well get on with it. Love and be damned!"

"What?" he repeated, surprised at her exclamation.

"It's a quote," she said, "from a film. And it seems apt for you."

He opened his eyes in confusion, then frowned as he realized she had a point.

"Darling Cam," she said more softly now. "I thought you had stayed overseas because of your passion for your work."

"I had!" he said indignantly. "I moved around a lot. Having a home was never an option."

"But it is now, isn't it? There's important work you could do here, in New Zealand."

"How do you know?"

"Zane told me," she said.

Of course. In Akaroa, no one's business was ever private.

"He shouldn't have. Nothing is settled yet."

"But it should be. Tell me, Cam, what's holding you back? It's clear that Belendroit is more home to you than to any of us, and it's pretty important to us. It runs deeper with you, this place, this land. Just like it did with Mum. Why can't you accept that your future is here?"

He jumped up and moved away from her. "Because it isn't."

"It's Charlotte, isn't it?"

He had his back to Amber, so he was able to close his eyes without Amber noticing, as a vision of Charlotte's beautiful face filled his mind. He gripped the sides of the kitchen bench.

He made some grunting noises as he tried to utter a few words—anything that would divert Amber—but it didn't work.

"Isn't it?" she insisted.

He nodded, jerking his head. "Yes, I guess it is."

"No guessing required. You love her and she loves you."

He sighed. "And therein lies the problem."

"Doesn't sound problematic to me."

"That's because you see things more simply than me."

"Are you saying I'm simple?" An edge had crept into her tone. She shrugged. "It doesn't matter. I probably am compared to you and thank goodness for it. I'd hate to be you."

He turned suddenly at this comment, which sounded as close to an insult as anything Amber would say.

"Why?"

"Because if you want something, you somehow, perversely, believe you should turn your back on it. That's weird, it's masochist and doesn't lead to a happy life. And I, unlike you, brother, want a happy life."

His frown deepened. "I don't want an *unhappy* one."

"Then what kind of life *do* you want?"

He opened his mouth to speak but couldn't find the words for once. How could his kid sister do what no one else could—get to the heart of the matter?

He shrugged. "I don't know."

"That's a cop out, Cam, and you know it. You *know* everything. You should turn your big brain onto your own life for once. Make a study out of that!"

Anger spouted from nowhere. "Haven't you got anyone else you can harangue, Amber?"

She folded her arms and had an annoyingly satisfied look on her face. "No."

"Aren't you going to stop?"

"No, not now. I'm getting somewhere. You're angry. That's good."

"Why is being angry good?"

"Because you're rarely angry and it's a sign that I'm getting to you."

He swore under his breath in frustration, and also recognition that he knew she was right. But he didn't want to go there.

"And don't swear, Cam."

He swore again. "What does it take to get you off my back, Amber?"

"You, acknowledging the truth. Tell me what you feel for Belendroit."

He looked bleakly around the room and out the window. It was as if he felt echoes, ghosts of his past and present here. Could he see his future, too? He closed his eyes. No, but he could feel it. He felt his muscles and mind relax as a feeling of rightness consumed him. "It's the one place which feels like home."

She nodded. "Good. Now tell me why you don't want to stay here." It wasn't a question, it was an instruction. Not for the first time, Cam thought Amber had missed her vocation. She should have been a counsellor. After all, she worked as an informal counsellor to half the people of Akaroa who came by her café or who bought her artwork.

"Because I don't want to *feel* anything, let alone feel that my home is here. That's the worst."

"Why? What's going to happen if you feel?"

"I lose control."

"And that's bad because?"

He pushed his hands through his hair and twisted in his chair. "Christ, Amber! Can't you leave it?"

"No, I can't. But I will *help* you out. You're afraid to lose control because maybe you'll allow the passion you devote to your work—something which you *can* control—to take over your emotions for a place you don't own, for a person who might leave. You can't bear to feel the loss. You feel it more keenly than most people and you're terrified. Just as Dad said. Have I missed anything?"

He sat back down in the chair, shook his head, and pinched his nose between his hands. "I can't bear the thought of going back to that time after Mum died."

"We all felt it," said Amber softly. "But you felt it more than most. You're different from the rest of us. More intense. But you can't go on avoiding feelings of love and belonging. It's not natural."

"For you, maybe."

"For you, too." She squatted awkwardly before him and took hold of his hands. "Open up your heart, Cam, please. Not for anyone else, only for yourself."

He knew she was right. He couldn't go on as he had been. With each passing year, each new place in which he'd lived, each passing, shallow relationship, he'd grown more and more dissatisfied. He *had* to risk it.

He reached out and ruffled her hair. "For someone who doesn't consider herself to be smart, you're the smartest person I know."

But she didn't react. "Will you change, Cam?"

He nodded. "I'll try. I know you're right. I can't carry on as I have been. There are two things which have got to me, prizing my heart open."

"What are they?"

"Here, Belendroit." He hesitated.

"And?"

"Charlotte." He was silent as they looked at each other. "The moment I saw her, I knew she was someone special. Someone for me. And each moment I'm with her, the feeling only deepens. That's why I left so abruptly yesterday."

"You've got some groveling to do," said Amber seriously.

He smiled. "I have." He got up. "And I'll start this evening. I'm taking the carol singing practice."

"I thought Gabe was."

"He had something else on."

"Good," said Amber, before turning away, with her hands around her stomach and a satisfied smile on her face.

What Cam didn't tell Amber was that Gabe didn't have anything else on. Cam had asked him if he could do it because, unbeknownst to Amber, Cam had already decided he couldn't have a future without Charlotte.

May the world protect him from well-meaning sisters.

❦

CHARLOTTE WIPED off the lipstick she'd only just applied and changed her dress for jeans and a plain navy shirt. She pulled her hair back into a ponytail and pulled a face at herself in the mirror before turning away. What was she doing? She'd changed twice already. She was jumping around, her frayed nerves making her snap at her assistant in the office, and miss a meeting. All she could think about was that she'd agreed to go to Belendroit and Cam would be there. It was hardly going to be romantic, not at all difficult to avoid him. Half an hour, a brief rehearsal, make sure everything was in place for Christmas Eve. Easy.

She jumped at a banging on the door, her reaction emphasizing the fact that the next few hours would be anything but easy. She paused, took a deep breath and opened the door to find the smiling face of Flo, complete with padded bags from which the most delicious smells wafted.

"Hey, Charlotte!" said Flo. "Thought you might like some extra goodies for when your dad comes. I know you hate cooking. The pudding and pies have enough alcohol in to keep for weeks."

"That's very kind of you," she said, puzzled by Flo's unscheduled visit.

"Not really. I've also been sent here to give you a lift to Belendroit. Cam was worried you wouldn't show up."

"He was?"

"Sure, he was. He's keen on you. You should know that."

"He's got a strange way of showing it," retorted Charlotte, following Flo into her cozy living room. Flo looked around with wide eyes as she placed the boxes of baking on the antique oak table.

"I've been dying to have a look inside your cottage. I didn't believe Rachel when she told me where you lived."

"Ah, of course not. Why would Miss Perfect live here?" She shot Flo a wry smile and Flo, looking embarrassed, turned away.

"Who told you that?"

"Doesn't matter. I don't think anything is a secret in Akaroa."

"True." Flo unpacked the bags and produced instructions for warming the contents, which she held up to Charlotte, who was notoriously unable to cook, before placing them on the plate. "But I got it wrong."

"I'm not perfect?"

"The image you show the world is perfect, but inside you're just like anyone else."

"That bad, huh?"

Flo shot her a knowing look. "Oh, yes. Anyway, I guess it's time to get going. You ready?"

"As I'll ever be," replied Charlotte, grabbing her bag and following Flo to her car. She was pretty sure that she'd never be completely ready to confront Cam Connelly.

CHARLOTTE FOLLOWED Flo around the side of Belendroit toward Lantern Bay. She hadn't been around the beach side of the house before and was immediately struck by the beauty of the beach close up. The pohutukawa trees arched over the sands and jetty protectively, the lamps which hung amongst them illuminated the intricate tracery of their gnarled branches. On the sandy shore of Lantern Bay, the carol singers stood fidgeting as Cam talked to a photographer who was testing the light. The occasion was being used for publicity, hence Belendroit and the sunset behind the choir.

Jim and Amber were seated on beach chairs, in lieu of an audience. Amber jumped up and waved for Charlotte to join them. Charlotte took a seat and, after exchanging a few pleasantries, sat back and listened to Amber and Jim's eccentric conversation. The shadows were lengthening in the garden but the insects droned sleepily, full with nectar and honey, and fantails darted about under the trees which protected the garden like a sheltering cloak.

It looked perfect. The kids looked gorgeous, Flo was so organized and Cam was a calm authority figure in their midst. One quiet word from him and they all stopped talking. Even Flo, which Charlotte was amused to see. With a raised finger, the children began to sing. But it wasn't what Charlotte had expected. She'd mentioned several times to Cam that she didn't think the pukeko song was appropriate, and she'd thought his answering smile had signaled agreement. Apparently, it hadn't. Her father would be listening to this, and she knew he'd hate it. He was big on tradition. Preferably English tradition.

There was no partridge in a pear tree, only a pukeko in a ponga tree. She could feel the tension in her stomach tighten as the kids reached the third verse. What would her father think? He was a New Zealander but with a heart firmly set in England where his family came from. She couldn't bear him to criticize anyone here. Maybe she could persuade Cam to do the traditional version?

She walked up to them as they finished the song and joined Flo in applauding them. By this time Boo and Stanley —Jim's cocker spaniels—had followed her and were barking at a stray cat. A car of teenagers stopped and shouted to their siblings who were singing. From somewhere inside the house, a baby—Maddy and Gabe's, Charlotte guessed— began to cry. Charlotte couldn't imagine a scene less like the peaceful, traditional Christmas she'd envisaged for her father.

"That's great, everyone," said Charlotte. "Well done."

"There's hot chocolate inside!" called out Flo from the house.

After everyone had gone, while Cam was putting things away, Charlotte plucked up courage. "I was just wondering…"

Cam looked at her with a wry smile, as if he knew what was coming next. "Yes?"

"Whether it wouldn't be better to sing the other version of Twelve Days of Christmas. You know, the usual version."

He hesitated for a fraction of a moment, then continued with what he was doing. "The usual version. This *is* the usual version for most of these kids. It's what they sing at school."

"Really?"

"Yes, really. So why do you think it would be better to sing the other version?"

She shrugged. "Just, you know, because…" She couldn't tell him.

"Because your father will be here." He gave her his full attention. "Because you think he won't approve of this version."

"Well, yes. I'm sorry, I shouldn't have said anything. It's just…"

"Just that you want to humor him. I get it, even if I don't like it."

"Cam, he's the only family I have. Of course I want him to enjoy himself. Anyway, I don't see why you're so worried. You've made it clear you're out of here as soon as possible."

"Ah, about that."

She folded her arms and raised an eyebrow. "You want to talk about that? Really?"

"Yes. I'm sorry—"

She waved her hand. "No need to apologize to me. To your family, maybe, but not me. Your future is nothing to do with me."

"Isn't it?"

"No. You made that quite clear." Despite her words, she could feel the anger drain from her. It seemed it didn't run deep.

"I want to apologize, Charlotte. I hadn't felt that way since Mum died and seeing Dad like that. Well, it just got to me."

"So every time you feel upset, you're going to walk out?"

"No. Never again."

"Huh! I'll believe that when I see it."

"You *will* see it. Because I've decided to stay."

She shook her head as her heart raced. She'd dreamed that he'd say such things. Had she imagined it? "What?"

"I said, I've decided to stay."

"Is this on a whim? Because you feel pressured?"

"I *do* feel pressured, but I can withstand any amount of pressure, believe me."

And she did. She nodded. "Why the sudden turnaround? Is it staying at Belendroit? It's clear you love the place."

"I do love it. But that's not why I'm staying."

She licked her suddenly dry lips. "Then why?" She was sure he could hear the hammering of her heart.

"Because I want to be with you. If you'll have me. Charlotte, I can't bear the thought of leaving you—of not having you in my life."

She felt desperate to hang on to something to protect herself. It was so sudden. From nothing to this. She shook her head.

"Am I imagining this scene?"

"No. I'm here, now, and telling you I'm going to stay because I want to be with you."

"You can't stay because of me."

"Why? I don't believe I've imagined how we feel about each other, have I?"

She refused to answer. "But what if we do... hypothetically—"

"Hypothetically," he repeated with a smile.

"Get together, and then split up. I mean, it's likely, isn't it? We've only known each other for a few weeks. Chances are we'll separate. Do you really want to stay on that basis?"

"You're right. Chances, probabilities, statistically we're bound to separate."

"Well then, I think you shouldn't make your decision based on us then."

"I don't have any other choice. Because science doesn't come into this."

"But, Cam, we're not good together! For goodness' sake! You've only just stopped calling me Charlie. And, I know it's weird, but I still think of you as Cameron. It's such a lovely name. But no one else calls us these names. They aren't who we are. We both want and expect something different from the other. That's no good."

"Charlie, Charlotte, Lottie." He sighed. "What's in a name? The only Shakespeare quote I remember explains it. 'A rose by any other name would smell as sweet.'" He waited as if expecting some kind of impressed response. But he wasn't about to get that from Charlotte. She'd hated studying English literature at school and didn't know what he was talking about.

"It means," he continued, "that it doesn't matter what you call a thing, it's still the same thing."

"Oh," she said, his argument pricking hers and deflating it instantly.

His fingers swept her cheeks. "I only called you Charlie

because I could see there was another you hiding behind Miss Perfect."

"Miss Perfect," she repeated softly.

"Flo used to call you that. Still does, although she tries not to."

Charlotte nodded. She knew already.

"And you calling me Cameron. It was…" He trailed off.

"Go on," she urged.

He let out a deep sigh. "My mother used to call me Cameron. And you calling me by the same name reminds me of the person I was, before Mum died, before I began moving around, refusing to settle. Before I began avoiding feeling anything that might hurt me. That's all we've been doing. Prodding each other to reveal our true selves."

"Put it like that and it seems almost rational."

His face moved closer to hers until all she had to do was tilt her head up to brush her lips against his. She didn't have to, because his mouth was upon hers before she could respond. And the kiss was different to any that had gone before. It was as if the shields had dissolved and there was only him and her, not fighting or resisting anymore. Not scared anymore.

Maybe, just maybe, they had a future together.

11

When Cam said he'd do something, it seemed he really did do something. Because the following morning, Charlotte opened the door to find Cam, Etta, Aimee, and Oliver—Flo and Rob's son—at the door.

"Morena!" greeted Etta, stomping into the small hall, dressed in black shorts and a black singlet which revealed tattoos which Rachel had failed to talk her strong-minded daughter out of. She clomped down the hall in her Doc Martens, carrying boxes of decorations, closely followed by Aimee, who held the neighbor's white kitten who was doing his level best to escape Aimee's embraces. Oliver followed carrying some things which Flo had wanted him to bring around. By the looks of the antique cake tins, yet more food was inside. Flo was utterly dependable for just about everything—especially food.

"Hiya!" said Aimee, lifting her cheek for Charlotte to kiss. Aimee was Cam's big sister Lizzi's daughter and as sweet and trusting as Etta was bolshy and boisterous. Despite their differences the two got on famously. And, somewhere in between, Oliver filled the gap. Oliver was Flo's stepson since she'd married Rob Connelly.

"Hello, Charlotte," said Oliver in his very proper English accent. His serious demeanor and timidity was slowly being chipped away by living with the Connelly and extended families. But he still stood out for his differences. Lucky for him, the Connellys had always embraced difference and they'd welcomed him into their fold as if he'd never been away.

"Hi there, Oliver. What have you got there?"

"Greenery for the summer house. I cut it myself. And biscuits, a cake, some decorations—Kiwi ones. Flo didn't think you'd have the right kind."

"Oh," said Charlotte, frowning. She wasn't used to being perceived as lacking anything. And with a glance at the decorations she realized that the few tasteful decorations she'd bought from an upmarket interiors store in Christchurch, and which she'd placed in subtle groups on the mantelpiece, wouldn't fit the whole Kiwiana theme conceived by Cam. She was fighting an uphill battle. "Oh, well, thanks. That's great."

Cam brought up the rear, taking advantage of the children disappearing into the kitchen to give Charlotte a long, lingering kiss.

"Hm, do you think they'd notice if we went upstairs? We could say we're decorating the bedroom."

Charlotte laughed, pushing him away. "That might work with Aimee and Oliver, but Etta? I reckon she'd come on up and tell us to get to work!"

"Ah, you could be right. My eldest niece is as sharp as a tack and not someone to mess with."

"You've got that right. Although I think she's finding her softer side, from what Rachel's told me." Charlotte heard Etta open the back door and take the others out to the small summer house which they'd come to decorate. "Apparently she's in love."

Cam gave a low whistle, and glanced out the window to where Etta was balancing dangerously on a post, reaching up to hang some lights. "And who's the lucky girl?"

"The girl we saw on the market stall. We'll get to meet her properly on Christmas Day at Belendroit. Etta is ecstatic because the girl has accepted her invitation for Christmas Day. Apparently Etta thinks this is significant."

Cam suddenly frowned and strode over to the back door. "Etta will spend the day in hospital if she's not careful."

Charlotte watched Cam call out to Etta, who ignored him, now lying on top of the summerhouse roof on her stomach, stringing lights across its front. The two younger children seemed more interested in next door's cat than decorating. Cam strode across the lawn and got the children organized.

Charlotte lingered for a few seconds before turning and catching sight of herself in a mirror. Her hair was tied in a ponytail and she'd caught the sun from some last-minute shopping she'd done that morning. She looked young. She frowned at her reflection. She also looked different. She walked closer to the mirror and knew where the difference lay—it was in the glow of her skin, the sparkle in her eyes. She was in love and there was no way of hiding it.

Smiling, she took a tray of drinks out into the garden and set them on the garden table. She'd offered her place as a stop on the route the carol singers would take because it had apparently been used for that purpose decades earlier. Her summer house could turn to follow the sun and abutted the reserve. It was the perfect place for a stage, lit by the evening sun and raised above the rest of the reserve. Cam was sliding the fence out of the way, and Charlotte went to join him.

"It makes the place look so different without a fence." She

stood on the edge of her property and looked out across the domain. "This fence couldn't have been opened for years."

"Flo said it hadn't been used for over ten years. But with Rob's help, I got it operational." Cam came and joined her. "I reckon your dad's going to love it."

"Is your dad going to be here, Charlotte?" asked Aimee, after giving up on the cat who sat well out of reach up a tree, tail flicking with annoyance. Aimee had a special interest in fathers, with her own having been distant after her parents' divorce, and with a new father, Pete, having stepped up and transformed her life.

"Yes, he is."

"That's nice for you. So you won't be alone in your cottage overnight on Christmas Eve."

Charlotte and Cam exchanged amused looks. Charlotte had no intention of letting Cam get away that night or any other night in the foreseeable future. "No..." She hesitated, but stopped herself from calling her father by his given name just in time. She didn't want to have to explain that to Aimee. "No, my *father* is staying in a hotel in Christchurch."

"Why?" Aimee frowned, her sweet face screwed up in distress.

Charlotte shrugged. "No reason. He'll just be more comfortable there, I think."

"Oh," said Aimee, but she didn't look reassured.

"It's okay, kid," said Etta, jumping down from the roof of the summerhouse. "Not all dads are alike. Some are more easygoing than others." Etta tossed Aimee a box of lights. She knew all about what Aimee and her mum, Lizzi, had gone through with Aimee's birth father.

"Pete's easygoing," said Aimee, the frown lifting from her face as she opened the box and disentangled the lights. "Mum's always saying that. She says she can't believe it. And

Zane is too, isn't he?" Aimee obviously thought it was the highest accolade anyone could give a father.

Etta choked out a laugh. "No way. He's as strict as. Anyway, Zane isn't my real dad. He's my step-dad, as well as my uncle. My birth father is Zane's brother. I can't hardly remember him. He lives in the US with his new family."

"Your family is more complicated than mine!" said Aimee.

"And mine," chipped in Oliver, not wanting to be left out. He was tying up bundles of greenery around the summer-house. Although Flo wasn't his birth mother, it seemed he shared her love of gardening.

"All families have their own complications," said Cam. "Charlotte's dad likes his space, that's all."

"But you've got enough space for us, haven't you?" asked Aimee. "Mum said we could all stay the night here."

"Of course." Inwardly, Charlotte was quaking. She'd agreed because she knew their parents wanted to be with Jim and discuss his care. But she'd been glad when Cam had said he'd help her out. She wasn't used to kids, but she refused to be daunted.

"Don't worry, Charlotte," said Etta. "I'll keep these two in line."

Charlotte shot Etta a relieved look and mouthed 'thank you'.

"Let's get some drinks," said Cam. As they walked back to the house, he said, "You're going to be fine. We're all going to be fine. Don't worry."

She opened her mouth to remonstrate but, after a kiss, she'd found she'd both forgotten what she was about to say, and truly felt that everything was going to be just fine.

AND IT HAD BEEN JUST fine. Now, two days later, as Charlotte looked around the house and garden which, between the children and adults of the Connelly family, had been decorated and prepared for the evening ahead, she felt a flutter of nerves. Why, she didn't know.

Everything was going to plan. She'd managed to restrain the children's attempts to decorate her house with the decorations remaining from the summerhouse. She'd been forced into a deal. She'd allowed the flashing lights, which screamed 'Merry Christmas' across her roof, but had drawn the line at the inflatable reindeer.

The food was all ready. She'd hired Flo to cater for the evening, knowing that her own attempts wouldn't be up to her father's standards. She inhaled the smell of coq au vin. Flo had laughed at Charlotte's choice of dinner for Christmas Eve. But it was her father's favorite dish, and he hated the type of buffet which Flo had initially suggested.

And she was ready. She'd waited until the last minute before dressing for the evening. It was only after Flo and Rob had left the food that she went upstairs to change. Not that there was anything wrong with a little black dress, pearls and stilettos, but she knew Flo would find it odd. Not to mention Etta. Not to mention, well, practically everybody in her new hometown. But it was only for one night. One night in which she wanted to show her father what she'd become—a successful woman. And, for once, she felt successful.

A sharp rap interrupted her reverie. Her heels clicked on the wooden floor as she went and opened the front door.

"Wow! Look at you!" exclaimed Charlotte with a laugh, as she opened the door to Cam, who stood on the doorstep looking as if he were about to step into a Monte Carlo casino. Sleek dark suit, crisp white shirt and a tie completed the outfit. She noted with approval that he'd even had his hair trimmed.

"The things I do for you," he said, stepping forward, putting his hands around her waist and kissing her deeply. "Um," he said, "perhaps we should go to bed. Your father won't be here for half an hour."

Charlotte laughed and pushed him playfully away. "William is always early. What on earth would he think if he came here and found us in bed?"

"That we can't keep our hands off each other?"

Charlotte rolled her eyes. "Strange as it seems, I really don't want my father to be thinking about such things tonight." She brushed her lips against his tenderly, wanting him to understand. "It's going to be a special night, Cam. The first time my father has visited me here. The fact he's coming means something."

He brushed his hand down her hair, his eyes roving appreciatively over her face. "What does it mean?"

"He wants me in his life."

"If that means so much to you, why did you leave Wellington? You'd have had more opportunity to be in his life if you lived in the same city."

"Because I needed to find a place for me. In Wellington, I was always my father's daughter, never me. I needed to strike out for myself, find my own community. And, at last, I think I've done it here."

"But you couldn't leave behind your need for your father's approval."

"No, I guess not." She shrugged. "That sounds kind of ridiculous for a woman my age."

"It's not ridiculous. We all have hang-ups based on our past."

"You think this is a hang-up?" She cocked her head to one side.

"Yes, don't you?"

She shot him a quick smile and closed the door.

"Let's get a drink."

"You haven't answered my question," he said as he followed her into the sitting room, where she had a bottle of wine chilling. She opened a cupboard and took out a couple of glasses.

"About my 'hang-up', as you call it? No, I don't agree. It's just a natural desire to be accepted by one's father."

"True. But a father's acceptance of his child is usually a given."

She winced and stood silently as he opened the bottle and poured the wine. She tried to ignore the hurt his words had created. His words had struck a wrong note, creating a discordance in the atmosphere which hadn't been there before. She forced away the idea. Everything would be fine. She took the glass of wine he offered her.

"You're lucky that you believe this is a given. In your case, it was." She lifted her glass to his. "Here's to this evening, and families."

He clinked her glass. "To families." He took her hand. "Let's go outside. It's such a beautiful evening."

Her spirits lifted. The strange feeling was aberrant. Everything would be fine.

Cam was right. It *was* a magical evening. The sun was low now and filtered horizontally through the trees, highlighting cobwebs and the underside of gray leaves, giving texture and depth to the old garden. She felt a fizz of both excitement and alarm at the evening ahead. She only half-listened to Cam as he talked about his discussion with Zane, who'd jumped at the chance to have Cam work on the Lake Waitahi project and others like it around New Zealand. He hadn't told the rest of his family yet about his plans. He planned to do that tomorrow. She suddenly realized he'd stopped talking.

"You are miles away," he said, his arms around her as they

both looked out across the domain to the harbor beyond. The lights, which had already sprung up around the town and the hills above, were reflected in the still, dark waters. Beyond lay Belendroit, its lanterns all that was visible amongst the trees.

"Just having one of those moments when you think about your past, feel the present is exactly right, and anticipate the future."

"That must be quite some moment."

"It is."

They looked at Akaroa in silence for a few moments. Then the sound of Christmas carols drifted across from the town where the festivities were well underway. They were scheduled to reach her summer house shortly. Cam glanced at his watch. "Your father's late."

A sudden panic shot through her, and she took his wrist and looked at the watch. Sure enough, it *was* later than she'd thought. She'd allowed her mind to drift and dream as if this wasn't one of the most important days of her life. She clutched her head and turned suddenly, searching the road for signs of the rental car her father was going to pick up from the airport. She'd offered to collect him, but he'd declined, predictably preferring the independence of doing it himself. He'd always refused, point blank, to be in the passenger seat of any car. For a moment, it struck her how alike they were. Then she dismissed it.

"He's late," she said in a ragged half-whisper. It was all going to go wrong. She knew it. That fluttery feeling she had in her stomach wasn't anticipation. It was a hint that things were going to go wrong.

"Don't worry. The flight's probably late. Let's go and check."

Once inside, Charlotte checked her phone while continually glancing outside when a car went by. She tried to access the app, but her hand was shaking. Cam frowned and took it from her.

"Let me."

She paced the floor but, before he could open the app, a ping of an incoming text sounded. He glanced at the preview and held the phone up to her. She took it from him, pushing the hair behind her ears as she tapped the screen and read the brief message.

It was as if someone had shot her down. Not someone. Her father. Her knees buckled, and she sat down.

"Why isn't he coming?" asked Cam in a cold voice, which she knew was controlling the anger he felt at seeing the message preview.

She shrugged. "He said something has come up."

He took the phone and scanned the message before handing it back to her. "He sent this after the plane had left Wellington. Like an afterthought."

She winced at the accurate observation. She couldn't bear it. She got up and walked away from Cam and his accusations.

"Aren't you going to answer him? Aren't you going to ask why, after so many months of preparation, he's not even going to bother to show his face?"

She turned on him, angry that he should attack her father, who must have had a good reason to cancel at the last minute.

"No. I will not contact him. Whatever reason he has for not coming is obviously valid. I will not hound him to find out what it is."

"Why not? In case you upset him? He doesn't seem to be bothered whether he upsets you."

"You don't know him."

"And I'm glad I don't. Because, Charlotte, everything I've

learned about him so far hasn't made me *want* to know him. In fact, it's made me want to steer clear of him."

"Then perhaps you want to steer clear of me, too. After all, I *am* his daughter and we *are* alike."

"Maybe you're right."

At that moment, the sound of children approaching broke into their argument, and they both looked outside.

"Let's not make the children suffer for your father's idiocy."

She opened her mouth to speak, but clamped her lips shut again and nodded.

"I'll go and slide open the fence."

"And I'll turn on the lights in the summerhouse. I can see people making their way here already."

There were more people coming over to watch the children who'd assembled ready for their piece than Charlotte had imagined. On the hour, Cam had the children in line, the lights, music and props ready to go. Charlotte wasn't required for the performance and so walked around to the rear of the crowd, needing to remove herself, to watch the scene as a stranger, as her father would have, if he'd bothered to come.

It was strange watching the children perform. Always in rehearsals, they'd been giggling, and something or other had gone wrong. But now it was perfect. They hit the notes beautifully, their combined voices soaring into the slowly darkening evening. It was a long twilight in Akaroa in midsummer and a magical one. Which made it all the worse for Charlotte.

The performance continued with a couple more songs until the crowd erupted in applause and, carrying lanterns, they continued on to the next venue which was by the sea where there would be hangi—a traditional Maori feast of food, which had been buried in the ground on hot stones, covered and then steamed for most of the afternoon. From there, the evening would conclude at Belendroit where Christmas carols would be sung until it was time to attend midnight mass.

Charlotte watched everyone drift away before she stepped back inside her garden. She walked around, picking up some of the litter the kids had dropped, feeling numb. She'd thought she was alone, but then heard the fence being pushed back into position and Cam emerged.

"Are you okay?" he asked, but didn't attempt to come any closer.

"Sure." She cleared her throat and looked away. "The concert went well."

"Yeah, the kids behaved themselves and got it right. A bad dress rehearsal and a good performance seems to have been right in this case."

"Yep."

"Have you contacted your father?"

She shook her head but realized he wouldn't see her in the shadowy garden.

"No. There's no point."

"I'd have thought there was every point."

"You don't understand. I don't want to alienate him."

"He doesn't worry whether he's going to alienate you."

Tears pricked her eyes, but she refused to cry. He took her silence for disagreement.

"I don't understand you, Charlotte. How can you let someone else decide your happiness for you? Isn't what we have, what you have all around you, more important? Isn't it enough to withstand whatever life throws at you? Because if it isn't, then maybe we don't have what I thought we had."

She felt torn apart and could hardly answer him.

"You don't understand," she said finally.

"I think I do. I'm right, aren't I? What we have isn't

enough for you." His voice was dull, dead, as if the emotion had been wiped out of him.

She couldn't find the words or energy to reply. They stood looking at each other for a few moments. Her heart was breaking, but her mind whirled with confusion. Who was breaking her heart? What did she want? Could she let go of things she'd held dear for years—things she'd been working towards all her life? Could she do a sharp about turn in her life's trajectory, not knowing what lay beyond it?

She gave a sharp shake of the head, and his face hardened and he took a step back. Without a further word, he walked away. She stood frozen to the spot. And, as the door banged shut, she felt as if she had fallen away from everything she knew and loved, leaving only emptiness.

12

*I*t was the sunshine which streamed through her uncurtained window which awoke her on Christmas morning. And it was the sound of children playing in the garden of the house next door which kept her awake. She'd opened the curtains of her small bedroom upstairs so she could see the stars. It was something she always did when she couldn't sleep. Seeing something out of her room, something far away, a universe in which she could forget herself, soothed her. But the hours in which she'd lain awake had been more than those in which she'd slept, and her eyes felt gritty with tiredness. And she felt plain sad.

She rolled onto her side and stared at the wallpaper—pink flowers on a silver background—upon which the sunlight played. The wallpaper was a bit of girly bling in the otherwise plain room, and she loved it. But this morning it seemed too bright, taunting her with its perfection. Nothing was perfect, not her, and not the world she'd created around her. At the center of it sat heartache just waiting to be exposed.

Her phone pinged with a message. She rose but didn't

bother to see who it was from. She'd replied to her father last night, telling him that that was the last time. There would be no further opportunities to get together.

She remembered the time when he hadn't been able to attend a school performance. He'd claimed he had a business commitment he couldn't get out of. After her parents divorced, she'd discovered that he hadn't come because he'd been with his lover. She remembered the time when he couldn't come to her graduation. He'd said he couldn't get away. By that time, he hadn't even bothered to come up with a reason. And then there were all the other times. Variations on an excuse. Variations given one time too many. Variations which all meant one thing—he didn't care. Her hope was extinguished now. Cam had been right. She couldn't keep hoping for a father who didn't exist. She couldn't keep needing his love and respect to fill the gaping hole inside of herself. Only *she* could fill that. No one else. Not Cam, not her family, not her work, not her community. She'd kept on running until she was here, in this moment, with only herself to rely on. Only she could do it. And she knew exactly where to start. Herself.

CAM RAN up the beach path, waved at Aimee and Oliver who were playing on the beach, and Lizzi, Pete, Max and Laura who were enjoying a coffee on the picnic blanket, amidst the paraphernalia of opened presents. Jim Connelly, now much stronger that his medication had kicked in, presided over them. Despite calls to join them, Cam waved ambiguously and continued on into the kitchen where he knew he'd find Rachel, hard at work, cooking Christmas lunch.

"Well?" asked Rachel, hands on hips, her face shiny from the heat of the stove from which emanated mouth-watering smells. But it wasn't food she wanted to discuss with Cam. She looked at him expectantly. "How's Charlotte? Is she okay after her father failed to turn up?"

Cam shrugged. "I don't know."

"Why don't you know?"

Her interrogation annoyed him, and he tried to fob her off. "Maybe because it's none of my business?" Strictly speaking, it wasn't. But it sure felt like it.

"Of *course* it's your business. It's patently clear that she's in love with you and that you're in love with her."

He glared at her. He didn't often glare at any of his sisters, or glare at anyone at all, but now he did. He wasn't used to people knowing what was going on inside of him, let alone challenging him, especially when it concerned emotions.

"Don't you look at me like that, Cameron Connelly!" said Rachel. "You can't pull the wool over the eyes of your family like you can everyone else, so don't even try."

Cam could withstand any amount of resistance from high-powered chief executives of international corporations, smooth-talking politicians, whoever. He had no respect for rank and status and he said what he liked to whom he liked, and could take whatever anyone flung at him. If he was right, he knew he was right and no one could change his mind. But, it seemed, his resilience left him when it came to his sisters.

He could feel himself crumbling under the onslaught. "I left last night on bad terms. I told her it was over." He uttered the last words in little more than a whisper. He hated that he'd done that.

"You what?"

"You heard."

"It's not over just because you said so."

He gritted his teeth. Admitting his sister was right, and he'd been wrong, didn't come naturally to him. And she *was* right. A long and sleepless night had proved that. What he and Charlotte felt for each other transcended everything and had to be fought for. Which was why he'd been phoning her, leaving messages, texting, since the early hours.

"I know. And I've tried to contact her, but she hasn't got back to me."

"But she *is* coming here today for Christmas lunch, isn't she?"

"I guess."

"You need to do more than guess, Cam. You need to go around and see her and check out how she is, and what she's doing."

Cam sighed and shook his head. "I'd forgotten how annoying it is to have sisters treating you like an idiot."

"We wouldn't treat you like one, if you weren't one."

He met her glare with one of his own. "I've just come from Charlotte's place. I've knocked on the door, peered in windows and had irate neighbors ask me what I'm doing. The only reason I came back here is because I thought she might have turned up."

Rachel frowned and tossed the tea towel she was holding onto the wooden bench. "That's strange. I wonder where she's gone? Maybe out for a walk somewhere?"

"Any other day, any other time, and yes. But after what happened last night? I don't know."

"Maybe she wants to be alone. You know what Akaroa is like on a sunny Christmas Day. Everyone is out and about."

"This is Charlotte we're talking about. She hates being alone."

Rachel bit her lip and sat down, looking worried. "I hope she's all right. She so wanted last night to be perfect for her father."

"I know. I guess she realizes that 'perfect' doesn't exist for anyone. Not for her, and not for her father. I have to admit, Rachel, I'm worried about her."

"Then find her. She can't have gone far if her car is there. Knock on doors, do whatever you have to, but please make sure she comes here for lunch. I can't bear the thought of her being on her own after last night."

"Nor me," he said, leaving the room. "Nor me," he muttered to himself as he took off on the coast path to Akaroa. First stop Flo. She had so many people coming and going through her house, she just might know something.

FLO WAS BUSY, as usual. She, Rob and their son, Oliver—after he'd spent the morning with his Grandad, cousin and aunts and uncles at Belendroit—were about to have Christmas lunch with her father, Ian, at her house, so she could also feed the waifs and strays who were staying at her back-packers and didn't have anywhere else to go. They'd be joining everyone else in the evening at Belendroit.

No one stood on ceremony at Flo's place and Cam walked straight through the open back door, greeting paying guests and friends alike who spilled out from the house, onto the deck and beach. He knew where he'd find Flo. The kitchen was at the heart of the house and Rob and Flo were both busy working side by side, putting the finishing touches to lunch. Although lunch didn't seem a big enough word to describe what Flo had on offer. Other people came and went, taking food outside to the long table which was erected in the garden under a pergola where it looked like around twenty people would be celebrating their Christmas.

"Hey there, Cam," said Flo, giving him a hug. "We didn't expect to see you this morning."

"I didn't expect to be here."

"What's up?" asked Rob, offering Cam a beer. He declined and decided to come straight to the point, not worrying who might be here. In fact, the more people who overheard, the quicker he'd find Charlotte.

"I'm looking for Charlotte."

"Oh," said Flo. "I thought you'd know. She came by earlier to borrow some things."

"What things?" asked Cam.

"Gardening things."

"Gardening things?" asked Cam and Rob in unison before looking at each other.

"Things are worse than I thought," said Cam grimly. "Charlotte's never shown any interest in gardening before. She pays someone to do her garden."

Flo's brow furrowed in concern. While Flo was the opposite to Charlotte in nearly every way, the two women had developed a bond and an appreciation of the other's qualities which had surprised everyone, including themselves. Flo looked genuinely concerned. "I thought it was odd."

"But she's not gardening at home. I've been round there. Any idea where she went?"

Flo shook her head and then stopped and looked up at him with a start.

"What?" asked Cam.

"She did mention something, now I think about it. She'd looked up to the hilltop there and said that when she'd first arrived and seen it, she knew this was the place she wanted to be." Her brow lightened. "Come to think of it, there is some activity up there. There's a community project to plant more trees on the hills."

"On Christmas Day?"

Flo shrugged. "Symbolic, I guess."

Cam nodded. "Thanks, Flo." He walked away before remembering, turning and waving to the others. "I'll catch you all later."

"And make sure Charlotte comes with you," said Flo. It

was the first time Cam had heard her call Charlotte anything other than Miss Perfect. It seemed as if nothing stayed the same. Not Flo with her fixed ideas about Charlotte, not Charlotte with her sudden interest in gardening, and maybe, just maybe, not him.

CAM DIDN'T SEE her at first. She was bent low over the earth, an old wooden trough of gardening tools beside her. Her hair was covered with a straw sunhat, but it was her feet which gave her away. The high-heeled wedge sandals were incongruous on the windswept hillside.

"Hey!" He greeted her from a distance, purposely trying not to crowd her.

She looked up quickly and then looked down again, finished doing what she was doing, and stood up. He immediately noticed there was something different about her, apart from the fact she appeared to be planting something. She wore old jeans, he noted with surprise. Jeans that were torn and too loose. And she was brushing her hands on them, he noted with even more surprise.

"I guess borrowing the gardening tools gave me away."

He nodded. "Yeah. Under harsh interrogation, Flo mentioned you'd borrowed some. I was worried. I mean, the idea of Charlotte, alone with gardening tools, I didn't know what to make of it."

For a moment, their serious gazes met before she burst out laughing. "I'm not surprised," she said, picking up her things and walking over to him. "I'm hardly known for getting my hands dirty."

"Nor are you known for being on your own," he said, falling into step with her as they walked over the top of the hill and looked out over the harbor. "Especially at Christmas."

She blinked as if he'd taken aim and found a sore spot at the word Christmas. "I've decided I need to be on my own more. Because you're right, Cam, I have to stop trying to heal me from the outside."

Any more thought of humor deserted him. "On your own?" he repeated. That wasn't what he wanted.

"Yes, it's the only way I can think of to deal with my issues." She raised her arms and let them fall helplessly to her sides. "I guess you think I'm pretty pathetic—a grown woman so needy."

He reached out to her then, hating to see her call herself that. "No! You're anything but. In fact, I'd go so far to say that you're the least pathetic person I know." He took her hand in both of his and held it tight. She did not remove it, which he took to be a good sign. "Never say that about yourself. You've spent a lifetime wanting something your parents should have given you."

"And I now realize that for the rest of my lifetime, I won't be searching for love. You're right, Cam. I have to be enough for myself, which is something I've avoided for too long. But all that's going to change."

"Good, I'm glad. You deserve to be happy."

"And I will be."

He tilted his head to one side. "You don't look happy."

"Not yet I'm not. But I'm determined to work on it." She glanced at the tree she'd just planted on the ridgeline. "Starting here and now. Putting down roots and watching them grow every day. That's my plan."

"It's a good one."

She smiled sadly, withdrew her hand, and they walked down the hill in silence. There was so much he wanted to say, so much he wanted to ask, but he wanted to tread carefully with this new version of Charlotte.

"And," he asked finally. "Do your plans involve coming to Belendroit for lunch?"

She grimaced. "It's kind of you all to invite me, but I'm not sure I'll be good company."

"Luckily, being good company isn't a pre-requisite for coming to Christmas lunch at Belendroit. Otherwise, most of my family wouldn't be invited."

She laughed like he'd intended her to. "Your family is wonderful. All of them. They're all so different, and yet they all enjoy each other's company."

"Because they love each other," he said. "That one thing over-rides everything else. Take Max and me. He's such a macho guy, and he underestimates the strength of others when it's not blatant."

"Like you," she said with a smile. "Although anyone who underestimates you will do so at their peril."

"True," he said, as they walked up to her gate. They paused there and spoke briefly to a family who were out with their children trying out their new bicycles.

Cam studied her face as she watched the family continue along the road, the father running to catch up with their toddler, who was scooting along on a trike. She looked wistful and unguarded, and he felt his love for her in every part of his body. It was overwhelming—both emotional and physical—and he knew it would always be there. And he also knew he'd do anything to make her happy.

She turned to him with a sigh, lifting her hand to shelter her eyes from the bright sunlight.

"I have to say I'm surprised to see you after what you said last night."

"I'm an idiot, Charlotte. I'm sorry, I should *never* have said what I said."

"You may be many things, but you're no idiot. You meant what you said. And you were right in what you said. I *was* letting someone decide whether I could be happy. And that's crazy. But, you know, that's not only about my father, it's about you, too. I can't depend on anyone else. Not my father, and not you. I can only depend on me."

Fear flickered in his gut. "You're taking my argument too far. I'm here, now, with you, and I know we have feelings for each other." He paused, wondering how far to go. "We have a deep connection. You're not going to throw that away, are you?"

She shrugged. "Honestly? I don't know. I have some thinking to do. That's why I chose to be alone this morning. And why I'll spend more time on my own—something I've been running from my whole life."

He swallowed. "Right. Of course. I mean, I think you're right. But…" He trailed off. How could he say that, while he was glad she was making changes and thinking of herself, he didn't want her to forget about him? How could he say that without sounding needy and a hindrance to her growth? He'd never been needy before but, then, he'd never been in love before.

"But?" she prompted.

He shook his head. "Nothing." He tried to shoot her a smile, but it slipped away too easily.

"It's unfamiliar territory for me, Cam, and new to you, too, I think. So how about we just take it a step at a time, and see what happens?"

He huffed a relieved sigh and raised his eyebrows. "It's a plan. So, can we take a step together and go to Belendroit for lunch? I know you want to be on your own, but you've got the rest of the day for that."

She looked doubtful, but smiled. "Sure. Otherwise, I'll have hell to pay from Rachel."

They both laughed, knowing that this wasn't true because

Rachel was one of the kindest, most giving of the Connelly clan.

"Do you want to come and wait while I get changed?"

He nodded. "Yes." He sighed. "Yes," he repeated after she'd left him to change. "Oh, yes." He'd waited a lifetime for someone like Charlotte. And now he'd found her, he knew he'd never let her go.

DESPITE HER DECISION TO spend more time alone, Charlotte couldn't help being cheered by the sight and sound of the large Connelly family milling around the old homestead. While the veranda was packed with Cam's brothers and brothers-in-law, the women could be heard talking loudly inside the house, and laughter drifted up from the beach. Only Rachel among the women was on the veranda. No doubt forced out of the kitchen to give her a break. It was Rachel who spotted them first. She grinned and held up a glass of fizzing Champagne in a silent toast.

"She's here!" shouted Rachel.

Aimee and Oliver looked up from a board game they were playing, while the others called out greetings. Jim awoke abruptly from a nap and proceeded to deny he'd ever been asleep.

"Did you ever doubt I'd come?" called Charlotte, with a confidence she didn't feel. With Cam beside her, they walked across the short lawn which led from the beach path to the veranda, where it seemed all the Connelly family had now gathered.

"Just in time," said Rachel, as Zane poured two more glasses of Champagne. Rachel held out glasses for both Cam and Charlotte as they walked up the steps to join the family. "Pre-dinner drinks. Happy Christmas!" She kissed Charlotte on the cheek and lowered her voice. "I'm so glad you came."

Charlotte gave her friend a hug. "So am I."

"I'm sure everything is going to be all right. You'll see."

A sudden shout from Etta, who'd appeared around the corner of the house from the beach, dripping from the top of her shaved head to her sopping wet jeans, turned Rachel's attention away from Charlotte, for which Charlotte was thankful.

"Have you got a towel, Mum?" shouted Etta.

"Look at your clothes! You're soaked. Haven't you heard of a bikini, Etta?"

Etta pulled a face, and everyone laughed. All the Connellys knew the chances of getting Etta to wear anything as feminine as bikini were approximately nil.

LUNCH WAS SUPERB, but Charlotte had expected nothing less. With two chefs in the family, it was a given. With Lizzi running The Lakehouse Café in Shelter Springs and Rachel fronting a syndicated cookery TV show, the Christmas lunch of seafood was presented with unusual sauces, and the locally grown vegetables and salad stuffs were used to create inventive and delicious salads with a definite international flavor.

But Jim had also insisted on a traditional barbecue, which went down well with the men. Rachel shook her head at the overdone steaks and the burned sausages, but Zane, Max, Pete and the children couldn't get enough of them.

And, more importantly, Cam had never left her side. Even after lunch, when people drifted into groups, Cam stayed with her, seemingly worried that she'd make a bolt for it. But she wouldn't. She knew he was right, that what they had couldn't be ignored. But nor did she think she could give him what he wanted. Not yet. And at some point, she'd have to tell him. She'd been stalling up to now. But she knew the time was getting closer. When he stood up and held out his hand, she took it and they walked in silence away from the veranda where Amber was talking to Jim and Zane, Pete and Max talked about some hunting trip they wanted to do in a few weeks while Rob, David and Oliver pored over some old books in a corner. The rapport David and Oliver had created the first night Oliver had spent at Belendroit had continued.

Charlotte went to walk down the beach to where she could hear Etta calling out to Laura, when Cam stopped and tugged her hand.

"I wanted to talk, Charlotte."

She swallowed and turned to him. "We've been talking all day."

"Not about the things which are closest to my heart."

She raised her eyebrows. "Your heart?" She laughed, wanting things to remain light, not wanting to tell him what she had to tell him. "Rumor has it that you don't have one."

But he didn't smile. "I have one and it's yours. Yours to do with what you wish. To hurt or to love. Which will it be?"

"Cam, I… It's not that easy."

"Sure it is. You either love me or you don't."

"Nothing's that black or white."

"Some things are. Like love. I had love here, growing up, but then I ran because the love turned to pain. And I've been running ever since. But I've stopped now. And I know, now, that there's nothing more important in life than love—that I've got to risk everything for it. Will you?"

"Honestly? I don't know."

"Hey, you two!" shouted Rachel. "Are you coming for a swim?"

Rachel ran up to them and put her arms around them both. She'd had a few glasses of Champagne and was hugging everybody.

"No," said Cam, unable to hide his irritation at being interrupted.

"Oh, look!" Rachel shaded her eyes as she looked at the jetty where Etta sat on the edge, her legs dangling. Beside her sat a glamorous long-haired girl in a pretty dress.

"Who's that?" asked Charlotte. "She looks familiar."

"That's Molly. Her family has just bought a holiday home in Akaroa. She couldn't come for lunch, but Etta invited her here this afternoon. Etta will be happy she came."

"Oh." Charlotte watched as Etta brushed something off Molly's arm and Molly turned to Etta with a flirtatious smile. "Is she…"

"Yes," said Rachel. "She's Etta's girlfriend. But don't tell Dad. We haven't told him that Etta's gay."

"Didn't he wonder about her changed image and her lack of boyfriends?"

Rachel shrugged. "No. I mean, neither necessarily suggests being gay. I imagine he thinks she's experimenting, or being creative."

"But he wouldn't mind, would he? I've never taken Jim to be homophobic."

"Oh, goodness no. But when it comes to your own grand-children, I don't know what his reaction would be. I'd hate for their relationship to founder because of it."

"Good Lord!" bellowed Jim, from behind them. They looked guiltily at him, having not heard him approach. Jim pulled off his sunglasses and looked over toward the jetty.

Everyone followed Jim's gaze to where Etta sat with Molly. Except they weren't just talking, they were kissing. And not just a friendly, platonic kiss, but a kiss full of tenderness. Etta had her palm gently held against Molly's cheek while her other hand held Molly's. With the children playing in the sparkling sea behind them and the family all around, talking, drinking, laughing, it was a beautiful sight.

"Oh," said Rachel, blinking back her emotion. Charlotte looked at her and saw her eyes were filled with tears. "That's so lovely." Then she looked at Jim, suddenly wondering as to his reaction. "Dad?" she asked tentatively.

"Looks like Etta has taken my advice," said Jim, beaming broadly and looking very proud of himself.

"What are you talking about, Dad?"

"My advice to Etta. I told her, if you like the girl, you need to make the first move. You have to risk everything for love."

"You know?" asked Rachel.

"Know what?" he asked.

"About Etta being gay. You know?"

"Of course I know." He shot Rachel an annoyed look.

"How do you know?"

"Etta told me, of course. We don't have any secrets between us. She's a wonderful girl. I told her, it doesn't matter who you love, just so long as you love somebody." He turned around to find all his family around him, having stopped what they were doing at his exclamation. "Just like I did with your mother. And just like you all did. You found the right person for you to love and be loved by. That's what it's all about."

There was a gasp from Rachel and mutterings from the others. Rob nodded, cleared his throat, and passed Amber a tissue for her tears. Lizzi put her arm around Rachel and they rested their heads together for a few moments. Both had been through so much and yet both had come through it all, and now had what they'd always wanted—a loving partner and children.

Max tried to disguise his tears by brushing his hands over his eyes, but he didn't fool anyone. Gabe looked out to the sea where Maddy was standing in the shallows, their baby in her arms. After doing a full circle of his family, Jim's gaze settled on Cam. "Isn't that right, son?"

Cam glanced at his father, his face serious, but his watering eyes revealing he was as affected as the others. "Yep, you're right, Dad."

"Etta told me she wanted to marry Molly," said Jim equably, as if Rachel's eyes hadn't widened with shock, and as if Zane hadn't choked on his beer. "And I told her, go ahead. Your mother and I hadn't known each other long before we got married. But we knew we loved each other, and that was enough."

"But, but …" spluttered Rachel. "Marriage? Dad. They're so young!"

Jim shrugged. "Young, old, what's the difference? Life doesn't stop after you're married. You still grow and change and develop. Difference is, you do it with the support of someone you love."

It was like the answer to a question which Charlotte hadn't asked. She turned to Cam and held out her hand. He took it instantly, and they walked quietly away from the others, out toward the small copse of woods which stood between the house and the road.

They walked in silence until they reached the beech trees, which provided shelter from the bright sun. The branches rose and fell gently in the light sea breeze, creating shifting shadows, and fantails flitted amongst the shadows, close around them. They stopped near an open trench, created by a team of archaeologists led by Maddy, Gabe's wife.

Charlotte drew in a deep breath, finding herself more nervous than she'd ever been. Cam had asked her once to be with him and she'd refused. She knew he was a proud man, and she had no idea how he would react to what she had to say. First things first.

"You are staying now, right, Cam?"

He nodded. "I've made a decision. I don't normally go back on my decisions." That was what worried her. "And nor,

I think, do you." But there was a slight raised intonation at the end, which made it more like a question. It was her cue.

"Yes, and no."

"Meaning?"

"Cam," she said, squeezing his hands tight. "It's true I need to stop depending on others to make me feel whole. I can't have my happiness depend on someone's approval of me. You showed me that. But—" She glanced across at Jim, where he was still enjoying being the center of attention. "But what your father said. It felt right. I don't have to do that alone."

His eyes immediately brightened, and so did her heart. "You don't," he repeated, picking up her positive note and refusing to let it go. "You most certainly don't. I'm here for you." He sucked in a stuttered breath, which made her realize exactly how unsure he'd been of her. "I'll always be here for you. Marry me and we'll have all the time in the world to live and learn together."

A myriad of thoughts flew through her head, taking her one way and then another. She knew she had a lot of work to do on herself to fill the hole of need that lay inside. If she accepted Cam's proposal, would she simply be swapping her need to be approved from her father to Cam? Would she become emotionally dependent on him? It was a risk. But as the thoughts left her brain, leaving only one constant feeling, she knew it was a risk she had to take. Because she loved him, body and soul.

She smiled. "Yes," she said simply.

Cam mustn't have been expecting her to accept, because he looked shocked, then delighted, then shocked again as if not trusting his hearing. "You'll marry me?"

"Yes," she repeated with a laugh. "Yes, please. I want to marry you. I want to live and learn with you. I want to be with you forever."

The word 'forever' had barely left her lips before he

kissed her. The kiss was cut short by a sudden shout from the veranda. They both turned to see Jim waving an overflowing bottle of Champagne at them.

"Come on, you two!" shouted Jim. "The Champagne is getting warm!"

Charlotte looked back at Cam with a smile. "All the time in the world," she repeated. "That sounds good, so long as you're in my life."

"I will be. That I promise. I'll be there for you as a friend. I'll be there for you as a lover. I promise I'll always be there for you. I love you, Charlotte, and I always will. You're a part of me now. A part of my world here, at Belendroit."

And, as they retraced their steps back to the house, which lay at the center of this large and noisy family, framed by a freshly flowered pohutukawa tree from which dangled the lanterns whose lights were dimmed under the bright afternoon sun, Charlotte felt, for the first time in her life, that she was truly coming home.

EPILOGUE

One year later

From her vantage point high on the hillside overlooking the harbor, Charlotte could see her old cottage below her in the valley bordering the reserve. And all around the familiar landmarks of other houses, shops, and the road winding its way out of Akaroa, up and over the hill, in the direction of Christchurch.

Shortly after they'd got engaged, Charlotte had moved in with Cam and Jim at Belendroit and she'd never been happier. Not that things had been easy. She'd been accustomed to living alone, doing things her way and living with two strong characters, they'd all had to give a bit. And Cam had been staunch in supporting Charlotte as she strove to be enough for herself—not for anyone else, not even Cam. Together, they supported each other and their love had allowed them both to grow. Grow enough that now she could face the fact that her father was coming to visit her with calm composure.

Her father had tried to make contact with her after he'd

failed to turn up the previous Christmas. But she'd cut all ties until a few months ago when, urged by Cam, she'd got in touch. She'd been surprised at how, prompted by her text, she'd received a video call from him and she'd seen how much her call had meant to him. It seemed she hadn't been the only one doing some growing up. She hadn't invited him to visit until now. But today was important—it was her wedding day.

She had no idea whether he would turn up and, for once, her happiness didn't depend on it. She understood him better now, and she still loved him, but that love wasn't a needy thing anymore. It was something which would always exist, but gone was the sense of emptiness which she'd sought to fill from outside of herself. She'd learned that it didn't work like that.

She reached out and touched the leaves of the tree she'd planted a year ago. The tree had withstood some fierce gales, and Cam said that meant the roots had anchored strongly. They'd penetrated the soil, forged their way into the earth, forcing it to yield as the tree gained traction and sustenance from it. It was strong now. It had survived powerful winds, periods of drought and prolonged rain, and was the stronger for it. Just like her.

She took one last sweeping look at the town of Akaroa, its harbor and the hills which encompassed it, before focusing on the twin-chimneyed roof of Belendroit. They'd be wondering where she was. She smiled and got back in the car.

Rachel and Amber were at the house waiting for her.

"About time!" said Rachel, stepping out from under the shady veranda. "I was beginning to think you'd be late."

"It doesn't matter," said Amber, kissing Charlotte on the cheek. "It's traditional for a bride to be late. And it would hardly worry Cam. He'd wait for you forever."

Charlotte glanced at the clock. She had plenty of time to get dressed. Everything was ready, because she had no intention of being late. Not today of all days.

"Charlotte." A voice said, which she hadn't heard for a long time.

She swiveled her head to the open front door and saw her father. She'd wondered how she'd feel when confronted with him. He looked older than when she'd last seen him in person, and a little less confident. She felt a wave of affection fill her. For all his faults and foibles, he was still her father. She looked back at Rachel and Amber, who were both grinning at her tears.

"Go on," said Rachel, her eyes misting over with tears. "I believe your father would like a few quiet words with you before the big event."

Cam Connelly felt more nervous than he'd ever felt in his life. He paced the short stretch of grass which led onto the private beach of Lantern Bay outside Belendroit.

All his family and friends were here. He'd had no regrets about staying in New Zealand. It was the kind of decision which, once made, seemed obvious. It was as if there could never have been any other outcome. He felt much the same about Charlotte.

He was proud of her, had watched her grow and change and become the woman she wanted to be. Quieter somehow, happier on her own than she'd ever had been before. They'd become engaged straight away, but he hadn't pushed her on a date because he knew she was concerned that she was using their relationship as an emotional prop. So he'd been elated and surprised when she'd broached the subject, setting the date for their wedding in the New Year. He still could hardly believe it.

"Cam!" shouted Max, his best man. "Stop pacing, will you? The nerves are getting to us."

Cam looked around to see Max, Rob and Gabe standing together, grinning, looking relaxed. And they should be, as joint best men, because it was their spouses who had their hands full. Laura, Maddy and Amber were busy corralling children while Rachel, Flo, Lizzi and Pete were busy inside the house with Jim, whose booming voice could be heard directing operations. Zane and David had taken charge of ushering people to the chairs laid out on the lawn, festooned with flowers and swathes of fabric.

"You don't look nervous," said Cam.

"No, but you are." Gabe, probably the least macho of his brothers, walked up to him. "Are you sure you're okay?" he asked quietly, so no one could hear him. The sympathy and understanding in his voice shouldn't have surprised Cam. After all, Gabe was Akaroa's favorite doctor.

"No, I'm not. What if she doesn't turn up? What if I rushed her? What if I should have given her more time?"

Gabe laughed. "It's been a year, and it was Charlotte who asked *you* to marry *her*, remember. And, besides, she's smart. Really smart. Smarter than you, mate. She doesn't make bad decisions."

"She does. Over her father, she did." Cam looked around. "And that's another thing. If he doesn't turn up, I swear I'm going to go to Wellington and sort him out."

Max and his other brothers heard Cam, and they all laughed, justifiably amused at the idea of Cam hitting anybody.

"Using your weapons of words, maybe? Anyway," said Max, glancing over Cam's shoulder, "it doesn't look like that will be necessary."

Max clamped his hand on Cam's shoulder. "No fraternizing with your fiancée before you get married. It's bad form."

"And you'd know, I suppose," said Cam under his breath, his eyes having shifted from Charlotte's father to Charlotte, who looked breathtakingly beautiful with her hair, left loose, flowing around her shoulders onto her gauzy white dress, which dazzled in the morning sunlight. "What with you having been best man to everyone here?"

"Yep," said Max. "I think I started a trend." He turned and signaled to the musicians, who began to play. "Come on, let's get started."

CHARLOTTE WALKED up the grassy path framed by trees from which lanterns hung, shifting in the warm breeze. Her father walked beside her, her arm resting lightly on his, and her future sisters-in-law and their daughters following on as bridesmaids. She glanced behind her at the women, who all wore their favorite dresses, as she'd requested. She hadn't wanted to inflict any particular style or color theme on them. They were all very different women, with unique styles and likes and dislikes. She had no need now to impose any sense of order around her. The only thing she wanted was for them to be happy—as happy as she was. And, by the looks of things, they were.

She looked straight ahead and then she saw him. Tall and handsome, his golden hair had grown a little longer now, just as she liked it. He looked like the film star his mother had once referred to him as. But he wasn't perfect and nor was she. But that was life in all its variety and it was a life she loved. And how much more perfect could you get than that?

~

AFTERWORD

Dear Reader,

I remember the first time I visited Akaroa. I was with friends, the weather was hot and sunny and Akaroa totally charmed me with its colonial buildings and picture-perfect harbor. I hadn't written any books then but, years later, when the time came to find a setting for a new series about the Connelly family, I knew it had to be Akaroa.

And so I first wrote about Akaroa in the last Mackenzie book —*Summer at the Lakehouse Café*—when Lizzi took Pete home to meet her family for the holidays. It seems fitting to finish the series with another family occasion—Christmas. Except, in this book, all the family have found the loves of their lives and are looking forward to a future filled with love, family and no doubt, some challenges. But there's nothing like a challenge to make you appreciate your family. I hope you enjoyed the book, and the entire Lantern Bay series.

If you'd like to find out what I'm writing next, you can

subscribe to my newsletter where I'll keep you up to date with my news.

Happy reading!

Sophie

Interested in reading more about the Connelly family?

Then why not start with Lizzi & Pete's story which is told in *Summer at the Lakehouse Café*—the last in the Mackenzies series (excerpt follows).

SUMMER AT THE LAKEHOUSE CAFÉ

BOOK 6 OF THE MACKENZIES—PETE & LIZZI

A staunchly independent solo mum. A winemaker who has lost his family. A summer in which to learn to trust again.

Lizzi Burnett part owns and runs The Lakehouse Café. But when her abusive ex-husband wants her to sell unless she can pay him out, she's determined that she'll do it her way or not at all. Because she refuses to trust anyone with her or her daughter, Aimee's, lives.

She won't even trust Pete, who she first meets emerging from the lake like a god—or at least like a kiwi Daniel Craig. Pete has re-located to New Zealand's Mackenzie country to start afresh. His family are all dead and he wants to move forward with his life... move forward with Lizzi and Aimee.

But what he doesn't realize is that the hurt he sees in Lizzi's eyes is only a fraction of what lies hidden, deep inside her. And it'll take a whole lot of soul-searching and loving to heal that...

Excerpt

Lizzi sat on the sand, and leaned against the side of an upturned dinghy, just outside the circle of firelight. Pete sat beside her.

"Thanks for inviting me, Lizzi. I realize you probably did it out of selfless pity for someone alone during a holiday weekend. And I'm afraid I accepted it out of a selfish desire to hang out with you and your family."

Lizzi paused. Why exactly had she invited him? "No, really, I thought it would be—"

"It's okay," Pete interrupted. "Whatever impulse made you extend the invitation, it's all right by me."

He looked straight ahead, over the flames toward where Max, Amber, Rachel and Gabe sat, laughing at some family joke.

"I miss that," Pete said.

"What?"

Pete indicated the group the other side of the fire pit with his beer bottle. "That closeness. The familiarity. The short-hand family uses, knowing that the others will understand.

It's a solid foundation of love which you take for granted until it's gone."

Pete rested his head against the dinghy, still looking straight ahead, his profile lit by the darting flames, the shadows they created revealing more of his strength than the most brilliant light could have done.

"I'm sorry," she said, wincing at the lameness of her response. She couldn't think of any words that could convey how much she understood and felt his pain. "And thank you for showing me what's in front of me, but which I hardly notice. I get so wrapped up in my own things. Aimee, the café, money…"

He turned to her then. "I don't notice *you* anywhere on that list."

She gave a brief laugh. "I guess I got left off so long ago I can't remember me being there."

"Then maybe you should add yourself. To the top, I reckon."

"I'm a mother," she said softly. "My child will always be at the top of my list."

As if on cue, Aimee left her position within Rachel's arms and stumbled over to Lizzi. "I'm tired, Mum," said Aimee, yawning, as she fell into Lizzi's lap.

Lizzi put her arms around Aimee and pulled her tight against her in a big hug. Aimee nestled into Lizzi's embrace, and Lizzi kissed the top of her head as Aimee yawned. She pulled the shawl from around her shoulders and covered Aimee who snuggled under its warmth. And there, at that moment, Lizzi realized the truth of Amber's words. She *was* lucky. And, she realized the truth of Pete's words. It didn't matter what else happened, she'd always have her family.

"Lizzi, what's up? Are you crying?" whispered Pete, his head close to hers. She pursed her lips and nodded, unable to stop the tears from falling down her cheeks, as both hands still held the now sleeping Aimee.

Pete brought his finger against her cheek and swept the tears away. He put his arm around her, and she leaned against him. None of her siblings seemed to notice anything was different. None of them looked at them askance. There were no raised eyebrows, or grins, to question her earlier assertions that Pete and she were just friends. They simply didn't appear to notice. Maybe they'd all got it right, mused Lizzi, and it was *her* that was slow on the uptake. Because being in the arms of Pete Marshall sure felt right.

Find out more!

ALSO BY SOPHIE HAYDON

The Mackenzies

A Place Called Home

Secrets at Parata Bay

Escape to Shelter Springs

What you See in the Stars

Second Chance at Whisper Creek

Summer at the Lakehouse Café

Lantern Bay

Yours to Give

Yours to Treasure

Yours to Cherish

Yours to Keep

Yours Forever

Yours to Love